P9-ARA-539

I am the beautiful stranger

Rosalyn Drexler

I am the beautiful stranger

Grossman Publishers
New York

Published by Grossman Publishers, Inc.
125 A East 19th Street, New York, N. Y. 10003
Published simultaneously in Canada by
The Musson Book Comany, Inc.
Manufactured in the United States
by H. Wolff, New York
Library of Congress catalog card number: 65–16854
The epigraph is from
Collected Poems of William Empson,
copyright 1949 by William Empson.
Reprinted by permission of
Harcourt, Brace & World, Inc.

For Sherman

LET IT GO

It is this deep blankness is the real thing strange.
The more things happen to you the more you can't
Tell or remember even what they were.

The contradictions cover such a range.
The talk would talk and go so far aslant.
You don't want madhouse and the whole thing there.

William Empson

I am the beautiful stranger

one

I feel so free. It's summer and I'm going to camp. Diana and Harry Felter go to the beach. They have a bungalow in the Rockaways, but they never thought of inviting me. Diana told me she meets lots of boys on the boardwalk. She wants to keep them for herself. Let her! I'll have friends at camp. But I wish she wouldn't say bad things about me to her brother, because I have a crush on him. A great big fresh fruit orange crush on him. He doesn't know it but someday he will.

:

Camp Bronx House is for kids who'd never see a tree. That's not why I'm going there. I want to find out everything. Before you can go away, the nurse examines your hair. She went through mine with a pencil but it was super clean. I wash my hair every three days. Once I had bugs in my hair and the barber shaved it all off; I looked like a prisoner. It was winter and I wore a hat indoors too. I remember that time very well because it was the first time I ever saw a hundred-dollar bill. Daddy brought it home and laid it on the table for Mom and me to see. He got mad because the table was sticky and grabbed the money up and put it back into his wallet.

What I want most is that when I get back from camp my parents treat each other different. I can't believe they really hate each other. Found six pictures of Mother with the heads torn off—she said Dad did it. It frightened me. I asked her why she didn't put the heads back on with scotch tape and she told me that he had thrown the heads away.

Mom knocked herself out ironing my clothes and sewing labels. I don't think I'll take any piano music, but the books I want to read and reread are *White Fang* and *Call of the Wild*. Hope I'm not unwell when I go; boys have X-ray eyes. I'm so happy I got my period. I waited a long time. Now so much will change—breasts, hair, and maybe my skin will clear up. Diana has always had a perfect skin. I'd like to bite her cheek and leave a mark there, but it would change into a kiss. I admire her as much as anyone else. Probably more.

Had to do time with Mom again. Dad at the drug store late. She bought me an ice-cream cone, vanilla fudge with sprinkles. Mom likes strawberry best. I don't like it—all those dead seeds crunching around on my molars. Ate the cones while we listened to Fred Allen on the radio.

I think that if I were a man I'd do better for a woman than most men (especially my father). I really hate him. When I tell Mother what I want to get her, she says she knows I will someday because I can do anything I want to do. She has more faith in me than in Dad. On Halloween we were buying a pumpkin in the fruit store—I was very happy. When we came out with the pumpkin there was a car parked in front of the fruit store. Mother seemed to freeze when she spotted the car.

"It's that redhead bitch!" she screamed. The woman answered, "Bitch yourself!" Mother took my pumpkin and threw it at the woman. It hit the side of the car and split open. The woman drove away. And now that my pumpkin is gone, how will I get to the ball? Just a joke.

I asked Mother why she was so mad at that woman and she answered that she was the one who hung around Daddy's drug store. "So what?" I said. Mom turned to me, red in the face, and whispered, "I caught them kissing in the phone booth." I was sure she was wrong, because Daddy would never kiss a stranger.

two

Diana Felter brought me a gift from her brother. It was the kind of snotty thing he would think of. I got so happy at the wrapping, rainbow tissue paper with a big pink bow. She said to read the note inside, and it said: "A talisman for you to carry forever." Before I even opened the package I swore I would. And Diana waited for me to see it. Harry had given her orders to watch my reaction and report back to him. I closed my eyes and peeled off the paper. It was heavy. It was a rock. Just an ordinary rock from Van Cortlandt Park.

"I hope he didn't go to too much trouble to get me this," I said. "Tell him it's the one thing I've always wanted."

"It was his idea," she said. "I don't care if you throw it at his head."

"Diana, this shows me how little you know about me. I love it." And I began to really love it. I put it on my night table to look at. Diana stayed around a while discussing how great graduation had been for her. (Dad didn't let me wear lipstick.) But I could tell she wanted to run off and make up a story about how bad I felt to her handsome sheik of a girl-hating brother. I don't get many gifts. Some of them are jokes. My father once gave me an empty box for my birthday, and then ten minutes later pulled out the real gift, an identical box with a ring in it. I don't understand joking around. I took that ring, and it was marvelous, like a flake of moth crystal dyed green, and I stamped on it.

"She's crazy again, Hannah!" he shouted to my mother.

I haven't been crazy often. Only on special occasions. Like before graduation, when I couldn't stop crying. It makes me think that I react opposite to the way I feel.

I'm a lucky girl of thirteen. A teen at last. I got into the hardest school to get into outside of Bronx Science: MUSIC AND ART. Now my friends should realize I'm superior, but it's me I can't convince. I spent three hours getting ready to appear at dear old P.S. 80. Ugly dress, ugly hair, ugly flowers, ugly thoughts, but I was on the program to sing "A Heart That Is Free." That's what made me cry. I realized that my heart wasn't free, and that I didn't even know what free was.

Maybe free is changing things around, like about this rock I was disappointed to get. I never thought of taking a piece of park and keeping it for my own personal use. Harry made me think of it. NOW I'll laugh in his face (if I can ever look directly into it). What's holding me back is I don't want him to look into my face and see that I love him.

Questions for myself: did he find the rock first by stumbling onto it, or, did he go out looking for it? What I want to know is: what came first, the rock or Selma?

The rock weighs about half a pound. It is irregular in shape and sparkles. When I look up what 'talisman' means I'll know whether or not it *is* one. I'm going to start taking it with me wherever I go: first to camp, where it may find its mommy and daddy, the earth and a mountain. I should compose a thank-you note to Harry: Dear Harry, Unknown to you, the rock you sent contained diamonds. I am willing to share this find with you provided that we remain partners throughout and you don't let anyone else in on the deal. Our business requires frequent meetings under cover of dark; but have no fear, the rock burns brightly and we will find our way. Sincerely, Selma.

TALISMAN: amulet; charm.
AMULET: a charm to be worn.
CHARM: magic spell; thing worn to avert ill luck or bring good luck; to delight; that which fascinates control by incantation.

If I were to wear my talisman and go swimming with it around my neck I'd drown. How would this avert ill luck? Once you're dead, luck doesn't count. I admit the rock fascinates me and I believe it's going to take care of me. I'm not a rock collector; this is the only rock that interests me.

FAMILY GROUP

A Play

MOTHER: What's this?
ME: A rock.

MOTHER: You'll scratch your desk.

ME: I'll put it in my drawer.

MOTHER: It's got dirt on it.

(LUCILLE *enters. She is eight years old. My sister.*)

LUCILLE: She kissed it. I saw her kiss it.

MOTHER: Why did you kiss it?

ME: What do you have against a rock?

MOTHER: You're crazy again. Throw it away or I'll call Daddy.

ME: Call him if you want to start something.

MOTHER: I don't start, you start.

ME: I'm saving it. It's part of when the earth was young.

MOTHER: At least wrap it in wax paper. I never knew you were scientifically inclined.

ME: There's a lot you don't know and I'm the first thing.

MOTHER: Shut your mouth and keep it shut.

ME (*singing*): "Fools rush in, where angels fear to tread."

(MOTHER *and* LUCILLE *leave, not being able to stand the noise.*)

I slipped the rock into a nicely ironed blouse in my camp trunk. I hope it will be comfortable there. Mother asked, "What's so heavy in there?" but she's weak. I don't think the trunk's heavy. When she saw me off at the bus she had to be funny: "Take good care of yourself and don't bring home any rocks, you got enough rocks in your head." She keeps telling the relatives about my head. It's propaganda. If your own parents think you're crazy, what'll other people think?

I want to say this one thing, camp was a good place for the rock. I mean The Rock. I half-buried it right by my bunk. Whenever I went in or out I touched its hard magic nose with my toe. None of the girls noticed, because in the country a rock's a rock. If I saw anyone else doing that, I'd wonder, but since it's me, I know, I'm casting a magic spell on myself. The reason I buried the rock is it belongs in the earth that created it in the first place.

Sent Diana a picture; it's real "cheesecake!" I'm only wearing a jacket (very short), and my knees are up. And I'm sitting on the grass with my face to the sun. My legs look fantastic, and I have a tan. It's my healthy look. I adore the way I photograph. If I'm lucky, Diana will show the picture to Harry. I want him to think of me as if I was a woman.

IMAGINE: I turn into a photograph. I'm smooth and shiny. I'm various shades of gray and black. Men pass me around and wish they knew me. Harry Felter keeps me in his wallet next to his G.O. card. I stay fresh in his memory. He won't give me up.

three

Camp kept me pretty busy. I didn't mind not receiving mail from Diana. I kind of enjoyed composing letters to her. I made them sound as if I was in a paradise. I described the flowers color by color, petal by petal, leaf by leaf; emphasized the soft green beauty of our camp lawn, and the sweet smell of new-mown hay: this in contrast to her hot sand and burning sun. I wanted Diana to know I had something better than what she had.

I might as well have one letter down here for the record:

Dearest Diana,

By now you are probably nice and tan. I have a tan too. There are lots of activities here. Yesterday I was in a play as a Greek goddess. I made my own costume out of sheets and pin needles. Every time I moved they stuck me, so it was hard to act mythological. I've passed the raft test and am now a "white cap," which means I'm allowed to swim out to the raft any time. Sometimes I'd like to swim all the way across the lake or maybe just to the middle and sink. But that's just an idea. Have you ever had the feeling that things were so great, so beautiful that you wanted to sink in and die? Don't, the ocean is worse than a lake and you may not be able to get back. I sang on talent night and am also writing a story for the camp paper. I met a girl here from another city, Albany. She comes from Albany but she's not an Albino (joke). Her uncle runs the camp and her name is Leila. She invited me to visit her in Albany. I think that's the way people should be. How is Harry? And what's he doing without his piano to practice? Collecting specimens for his microscope? I am enclosing a cut of my hair for his close inspection. I've been told it's extremely fine and won't hold a curl. I like my hair best about me. What do you like best about you: your eyes? Am also sending you the petal of a tiger lily (that's for you). Write and tell me what you are doing and if you have a new boy-friend. The boys here are babies.

Your friend forever,

Selma

Once I sent her a dead frog without a letter. I was so anxious to catch it that I hit it over the head with a milk bottle. I would have liked to watch her open that letter.

Leila gets letters from a boy she met in New York. He did something awful that she can't tell me about and now he writes to her from detention homes. I never met a boy like that. It seems exciting. I read his letters, and as soon as he gets out he's coming to see her in Albany. Perhaps we shall meet. I'll ask her if I can write to him too. It would be a welcome change to be better than someone else—more privileged, richer, smarter. I wonder what he sees in Leila. She's four-eyed and bow-legged and doesn't know how to kiss.

Got Leila to show me her letters during rest period. She made me promise not to tell anyone about them, especially her uncle who runs the camp. That's how she got in even though she's not a New Yorker. Her uncle pulled some strings. I think Leila has more "experience" than she lets on. Her big breasts are one thing in her favor. I copied her letters for my own memories; they made me cry. If I write to him maybe I can cheer him up. I am the beautiful stranger.

LETTERS FROM CHARLEY ROGEN

Dear Leila,

I hope when you receive this letter you are in the very best of health. As for me, I'm getting along alright. Well Leila, you ask me how it is up here it's terrible. For one thing its Boring because you see the samething over and over again. I sure wish I could get out of here. you know I've been here a month already, and it seemed to me like a year. Tell me something Leila, how did you past the fourth of July? I sure hope you had a nice one, with fireworks and all. Leila, over here I Past a terrible fourth. My mother tried to take me home, but they didn't let her. ain't that a "blip." tell me; how did you Past those red white and blue days that just Past. did you have fun? if you didn't to bad. I now if I was out I would of have a nice time. I would of "bomb" all of you girls. Leila I guess that's all I've got to say for now.

P.S.

Write to me.

Your friend
Charley (Chas)

My Friend Leila,

Well you ask me if one of your friend could write. "yes." Leila you said that you been writing a lot. if you think so dont write any more. I wouldn't mind if nobody writes. If I wrote something that dont belong here. dont mind it. that about it, Leila.

Sincerely Yours,
Charley Rogen

Dear Charley,

I'm the one who wanted to write to you. My name is Selma. I have blue eyes and dimples when I smile. Leila described you to me, so I know what you look like. To tell you the truth, I read some of the letters you sent her, so don't be surprised if I mention certain things. I'd like to be frank with you at the beginning of our correspondence. I'm not happy either, but probably you have more reason to be unhappy than I have. If there is anything I can ever do for you, please ask me, because then I'll know what you need. Do you know what you want to be when you grow up? I want to do so many things that I'm confused. I sing but I don't like to sing for people. Sometimes I write poetry. Not the kind about blue skies either. If you want to give Leila a rest and write to just me, fine, unless she minds.

Sincerely,
your new friend
Selma Silver

Dear Selma,

I like girls with dimples, it makes them look cute. and I dont mind hearing from a friend of Leila. Maybe sometime you send me a poem but I gotta warn you, it better be good. You know what I think I do when I get out? well it is a mechanic. Cars get me whacky. Thats what I want to be, but it hard to get training if you don go to school. I hope you are in the Best of health, and Leila. I'm doing alright. Selma on Friday (Aug 17) I left the youth house (since you know about me from Leila), and they took me to Otisville. I'm not in Crestfal. I thought I was goin to Crestfal but I didn't. Leila I cant tell you much about Otsville, because I haven't been here long. Right now I'm in reception. I'll stay in reception for the first two weeks and then I think I will start work. they said up here that the average boys that stay here is about eight or nine month. I think I am one of those average boys. the address of this place is in the back.

Charley Rogen
P.O. Box 8
Otisville N.Y.

Well Selma that all I got to say for now, do you know you sound like celery?

P.S. Write as soon as Passible.

Stay real cute,
Charley Rogen

Dear Charley,

Sometimes eight or nine months isn't such a long time if you think ahead. The one thing is sure that if you keep busy, time will fly. We have a schedule up here, but it's all amusements, not work like you have to do. I love to dance; Leila says that you are a great dancer. My plan is that when you come out, and when you visit Leila, I'll run away from home at the same time and come and meet you. Leila belongs to a club that'll throw a party for you. You haven't asked me to do anything or send you anything yet, except the poem. Suddenly I can't write one, maybe because you said it had to be good, even if you were joking. I'm drawing a picture of the pine trees for you. Camp is surrounded with pine trees and right under them the pine needles are so thick it's like walking on sponge rubber. I lay on my back and wonder how it is to be caught like you. Would you ever let me know why you're there? I'm very sympathetic.

Sincerely,

Selma

Dear Selma,

Just a few lines to let you hear from me. I mean Selma, I hope when you receive this letter it fines you in good health. as for me I'm getting along alright. Say if you want to know so much so fast you better get wise, you won't like what you hear. so better wait till we know each other better. Most girls go for me but you sound different. theres a chance you wont care for me because in a way your just a kid (Leila told me how old you are). Still if you care to take a chance lets keep it this way. You said if I needed anything to dont hestate to tell you. Well, I got something in mind. It isn't nothing much and it isn't much to look at. I'm only kidding. Well what I had in mind is a picture. a picture of yourself that is. you see, the picture Leila sent me I lost. somebody took it while I was in the youth house. I had two fight in the youth house. that right, I did. By the way I had a bunch of fight not only two. you want to know how old I am. well I'm now fifteen and when I get out of here I'll be past sixteen. that sure is a long time. Selma, the song I hear up here that I like is drinking rum and coca-cola, and maybe and also tangerine. When you write tell me the song you like up there. so that when they come on the radio up here I can listen to them. do you know something I like the way you fancy your letter up. it a good thought but you don know how to draw, dont let that stop you. Nothing ever stop me. your pine trees make me feel like your *crazy*. I'm only kidding. I only wish I could fancy my letter up like that too. Selma I signing off. 13-14-15-16

Write soon,

Charles

Dear Charles,

I hope you are feeling fine too and that when you look inside this envelope it will make you happy. I have enclosed the photograph you requested. It's the sexiest one I have. Don't fall in love with me, though. I was in love, recently in fact, but it ended unfortunately. I have a souvenir, however, to remember him by. Do you save things? I save some things like pictures of paintings out of magazines. It makes me feel that life can be beautiful. Sometimes I get so dreamy I don't hear what people are saying. Maybe I don't want to. Anyway, I have a reputation for being a little nuts in the cocoanut. My secret fear is, and I'm telling you because I think you'll understand, is that, hold on to your hat, my mother and father will send me to an insane asylum. That's where they store the nuts for winter. Ha, ha. Joke's on me. My favorite song at the time is "Indian Summer" but I'm changeable. Have you heard "Chattanooga Choo-Choo?" It's a great lindy. Leila and I practice the "breaks"—I invented a few myself. I would love to have a photograph of you too. Familiar looks grow on you. I suppose it's stupid to say, if you get into more fights don't get hurt, but I mean it. I was once challenged in school by a horrible girl but I didn't show up (neither did she). I don't mind being a coward as long as I don't get hurt. By the way, why did it take you so long to write? Your letters are most interesting to me.

Your friend,
Selma (celery)

My friend Selma,

Just a few lines to let you hear from me. Selma, how are you feeling? fine, I hope. ask me how I am and I'll say O.K. you ask me why did it take me so long to write a little letter. Well, I'll tell you up here I've been doing a lot of work, and I haven't got much time to write and thats the reason why. you told me in your letter that you'd like a photograph. Well, I'm waiting for my mother to bring me my wallet. you see, I haven't gotten any visit yet. you ask me how many visit can I get in a month. Well, its once. That sure is a long time before you can get a visitor. Selma? why do I think you look like Ann Southern when you dont. I told you Otisville don't look like the Picture I sent you (did you get it? you didnt mention it). what does it look like then? Well it looks beat up. Well, you know that you'll get old and I'll get old, well, what I'm getting at is Otisville looks old. you know something that the last letter you wrote made me "crack" up, it made me crack up when you said that you were a little nuts in the coconut. Selma you look older than I thought of you in the picture you sent me. dont get me wrong now. I'm not trying to say your old but you know their was a record I didn't mention before when I wrote you. the record is, who's sorry now. its a tough record, you should hear that record. it made me feel bad. After all, who's sorry now? Selma tell me something serious. do you get tired of writing. if you do tell me so that we can write less to each other. be frank about it. I wont get mad. in fact I'll be glad for telling me the truth. if you do happen to say what I'm thinking, I'll understand. that one thing about me I understand everybody. that about it Selma. I'm signing off 21-22-23-24.

P.S. even if you dont write
I'll send you my photograph.
I'll tell you when I might
be out. it might be on March, April, May, etc.

From the one who'll never
forget you,

Charley (Chas)

Selma, I dont have any love for this place.

Dear Charles,

You're right. I don't want to write to you any more. I want to see you. I don't get tired of writing, I get tired of imagining our friendship. Anyway, I'm going home soon to the city and in the city my mail isn't private. I haven't been given a mail key. If Mother happened to read one of your letters, she'd tear it up. I've thought of having a secret box at the post office, but get stingy when I realize it costs money. Don't worry, though, remember our Albany date. If you write to Leila she can write to me and then I'll know when you're out. I hope it'll be closer to March than May. Who knows what's in store for us. Remember I told you I was once in love? Well, I still am, but I think it's possible to love more than one person. Do you? I mean in different ways, only why does it have to be a secret? By the way, Leila told me that another guy up there with you told her that you don't do any work up there like you said. Is it true?

Your friend,

Selma

Dear Selma,

Just a few lines to let you hear from me. Selma you doubted my word when I told you I do work up here. You said that Leila told you I don't do work. Well she's dead wrong if you want to know something, Leila never been here. I do admit I didn't do any work in the Youth house. And who's the guy who told her? I'll bet she told herself and you agreed with her. How do you know that when you never been here? Just in case you don't know. When you go to an institution you go on a tuesday or on a Friday. on tuesday you go to Lincoln hall and on Friday you go to Crestful if you are under 15. If your older you'll go to Otisville. Selma, I think it would be better (like you say) if you dont write any more. if you do write I won't answer the letter. When you go to an institution is not on a Wednesday.

From

Charley R.

four

I thought good things were happening everywhere because they were happening at camp, but when Mom and Dad met me at the bus, the same old thing: he was disgusting and my heart sank. I felt that no matter what good things ever happened to me it would still be me: the stupid little snot nose, the worthless shit, the ungrateful rat—all the names they ever called me or each other—because nothing ever changes, not even the face of things, it just gets older.

I forgot to mention the best thing about camp: food. Only once it wasn't so good when we went on a hike and I was crossing over a stream and fell into the water, lunch and all. Nothing soaks up water faster than white bread. So I shared Leila's lunch and ate more than she did. I watched the fish devour my sandwich and swim away under a cool rock, which is what I would have liked to do. That's the end of my story, which reminds me of that famous poem:

Tell me a story
of Jacky O'Nory
and now my story's begun
Tell me another
about his brother
and now my story is done.

Think I'll make up a poem about my sister.

Tell me a blister
of my little sister
and now my blister is closed
tell me a pusful
about how she's trustful
and now the story's exposed.

If she ever wears my sweater again I'll break her head. Nobody's going to call me selfish just because I don't want her to dirty my sweater. It doesn't fit her, anyway, and the more Daddy dear hits me for taking it back, the more I'll hate that freak with fourteen curls hanging off her head.

My worries are over. I'm leaving town. I'm leaving city and friend and foe and most of all family! They can't stand me? I can't stand them! Now sister Lucille can have both pillows and my share of food and all the books, and my left-over tickets to the World's Fair. Leila has written me a secret document revealing the whereabouts of Charley Rogen, who is back in Albany. She says he's dying to take me out. She also suggests a devious route that I must take in order to deceive the enemy. First order of the day is to borrow money from Grandma G. She doesn't need it. I'll tell her I want to buy Mother a present. Second order of the middle of the day, which it'll be by the time I finagle the money out of Grandma G, is, buy the train ticket. And then with light baggage and nary a fare thee well, I'll be off. Mother can tell the high school that I had to go to Florida for my health. She hates lying, I love to make her lie for me. We can get a doctor's certificate easily enough. Maybe I *am* sick. Why shouldn't I be sick. I suppose I should at least leave a note that I'm okay and will be back soon but "don't try to find out where I am."

Dear Mom,

I'm not doing this to worry you, but I can't stand living at home with the others who live at home. Consider this a bonus vacation I'm taking for myself. I'm fine so don't worry. And don't try to find out where I am, if you love me. Cover up for me at school, I'll be back sooner than I think probably.

Your daughter, I remain alive
with great effort,

Selma

P.S.

I may send for more money. I have enough meanwhile.

I am writing this on the train to Albany. I went to see Diana first, though. Her mother was braiding her hair. Her mother loves her. You can see it the way she enjoys doing things for her. She asked me if I wanted her to braid my hair too because it looked so wild. I said "No thank you" because I didn't belong to her. Later in Diana's room I asked Diana to braid my hair (because we belong to each other whether she's aware of it or not) and she said, very coldly, "I'm not good at it. Besides, it doesn't become you." Diana has lovely hands. She played the Beethoven Sonata in A for me before I left. Harry came in and closed the door to his room without saying hello. How can some people be so independent, or is it rude?

Some kids don't care if they just go away anywhere to no one, but I like to go somewhere to someone. When Leila invited me to visit her, she didn't think I'd take her up on it. Neither did I —at least not so soon. She doesn't even know I'm coming. It was a snap decision.

Bought an orangeade. My head itches. No fun to scratch: nothing to snap, crackle, or pop. The ugly sailor next to me wants to talk. The whole navy can drown, for all I care. The lights are dim now. He's pretending to be asleep. His body is definitely leaning on me. What can I do? Wake the potential hero up? His ear is right on my breast. It is a deaf ear, but that doesn't stop the breast from speaking. It will say something to anyone. Like the dog whose mouth waters at the sound of a bell, my nipples rise to the occasion at a touch. It's too easy, it isn't fair, it's not personal—boy, I'm empty, and I'm on my own.

I wasn't going to say anything about the Albany trip because I formed an awful picture of myself there. I mean I saw what a jerk I was pretty clearly, just interested in myself. Leila's family is poor too, and sad. First of all, the place they live in is rotting wood. You have to feel your way up a tall flight of splintered stairs, then there's a rusty screen door. When you come in the door, you're all the way in. One central room serves as a kitchen, bedroom, and living room. A pot-bellied stove warms the place up. Leila says you can get gassed from coal fumes unless you keep the windows open, and they do, so it's kind of keep warm and die, or, live to freeze another day. Her parents are suspicious of me, I mean me as a runaway idiot, not me as a mysterious spy. I believe they sent a telegram to my parents about where I was.

Leila was very nice to me. We slept in the same bed with her little brother Peter. I kept wanting to hug him but Leila was between us. Warm flesh on a winter night seems wonderful. It's something that kids with a whole bed to themselves miss. That's why they want to creep into their parents' bed. Why should they be alone? Daddy always used to lay next to me on top of the covers whenever I woke up with a nightmare. I just remembered something funny about him—how he took showers with me but wore bathing trunks.

I went to the toilet three times during the night because I was wearing a sexy nightgown. I hoped Leila's big brother Al would see me but he was really out. The dark room and the red glow from the stove might have seemed romantic at any other time, but to me, wandering among the bodies, I had a strong urge to get out of Albany.

Leila told me that Charley Rogen steals cars. He has a passion to go fast. His nickname is "Speed." I don't have a nickname because number one: my name is short already, and number two: I don't have a passion with an easy sound to it. Charley is known to put his foot all the way down on the pedal and not care. He starts cars without keys, and if he gets mad because the car won't start, he pours sand into the gas. That's one side of his character, the side that got him sent away; but it didn't cure him. Because I know personally, I was in one of his "special" cars. He has good taste. It was a red convertible with white-wall tires. We rode down the highway at top speed, of course, and he abandoned it near an old factory. He was wearing a leather jacket and new jeans which were very stiff. I casually allowed my hand to brush his fly to see if I excited him, but all I could feel was starch and a well-sewed seam.

"Don't never wear new jeans," he said to me.

Then we kissed and it was pure spirits of ammonia. I shuddered and my eyeballs pained me, my forehead scrunched down, and I gritted my teeth.

"Open your mouth, baby," he asked.

"I don't really want to," I said. "I ate onions tonight."

"I ain't fussy," he answered, and bent me back on the front seat. New cars are pretty comfortable. I didn't realize it. If I furnish my own home someday I'd like to get a red leather couch out of leather. But I didn't open my mouth, and he tried hard to press it open and bite it open and then finally:

"Say are you a bitch, a real cock-teasing bitch! Why'd you come with me if you don't do nothin'?"

"I like you," I said.

"You don't know what you like," he answered. "Do you like this?"

I had to fight to keep him from pulling my blouse off altogether. It had green leaves on it in dark and light green and was real Irish linen. As a rule blouses are terrible on me, but I wore this one out. Charles tried to bite my buttons off. I think it was his idea of a joke. So I hit him with my head and we both went "Ouch!"

"You know somethin'?" he said. "You gotta hard head. It looks soft but it could hurt you."

"I've known that for a long time," I said, and then: "Let's go."

We took a bus back to Leila's and she asked me what we did and we had hot chocolate and I didn't tell her anything, so she imagined the worst. That put me up a peg in her estimation. She sneaked around to her parents' bureau (they were asleep, they go to sleep early, I think they're constantly asleep) and took out a plastic case about as big as a Swedish pancake.

"Look at this," she whispered, and I looked as she opened it up and showed me what seemed to be a large rubber bottle cap. "It keeps you from having babies," she said. I was amazed.

"What do you do, pray to it?" I asked.

"You wear it. You wear it inside, it's like a shower cap."

"Does it come in colors?"

I didn't want to be too interested. I also had some thoughts of my own about Leila and why she was so anxious to share this information with me.

I suppose her puky looks and four eyes fooled me about her sex life; she must give it away free on every street corner. She laughed at what I said and put the object back in its hiding place. When we got undressed for bed I watched her very carefully to see if her life left any marks on her, like fingerprints, or something deep like a prehistoric mollusk but not prehistoric and not a mollusk, maybe a tiny swirl of someone else's hair pasted to her thigh. I searched her all over but she was smooth ivory all the way up and around. If she was saving anything, any historic treasure from her eventful life, it was stored in her belly button, and that would be going too far to examine. So I fell asleep being the dirty one in the room.

Received a call from Cousin Lenny. My parents respect his opinions even though he issues them from between jaws held together with tiny rubber bands. His bite is off, and I might add he is too, or he wouldn't seem so sane. He told me to come home immediately and not make my mother sick. I told him to mind his own business. I like him, but liking him has nothing to do with the way he really is. He was nicer when we were younger; one Christmas he couldn't wait to give me my gifts—

rushed into the toilet and handed me a real bark canoe (toy) and a gray flannel bathrobe.

Naturally I came back, even though Lenny was the one who told me to. I had nothing to do in Albany and I wasn't really welcome. My parents seemed refreshed by my absence. They sure puzzle me. Shouldn't they be mad? I ran away and no one suffered.

Was my usual bitch self at dinner this evening. Refused to eat the liver, made faces, picked at everything till I nauseated everyone else. Mother kicked me out. I threw shoes and a flashlight against the wall of my room. (It's one big wall to me.) She came in spoiling for a fight and threw a dish towel at me. Not a very effective weapon!

In some way I'd like to make this next happening funny; it happened to me and it hurt and it made me hate. (Hate, kill, kill, which is the real gorilla, Selma or King Kong?)

TIME: four o'clock
WEATHER: miserable
PLACE: my bedroom
PEOPLE: Mom and me
REASON: fight (rematch)
MOTHER: You'll go if I have to drag you there.

ME: I don't want to.

MOTHER: You rotten pig! Put on your coat and come on.

ME: I'm very tired. I want to stay home and read.

MOTHER: Don't you waste my money. I'll break your neck.

ME: Go ahead.

MOTHER: If you don't hurry up you'll miss your lesson.

ME: Even if I go I won't sing. I'll stand by the piano and cough.

MOTHER: Cough? Cough? You'll be a bastard and cough when I'm trying to do you something good? I could use the money for myself but instead I want to make something out of you and you're going to cough and embarrass me to your teacher!

ME: Yes.

MOTHER: (*She punches me in the stomach and knocks me on the floor. She kicks me a long time and doesn't let me up.*)

Why did it happen? When she ran out of the house I pretended I was at my lesson and sang. I sounded as if I was rubbed out and something else written on top.

five

I had a gathering and we played that kid's game Spin the Bottle. Once the neck of the bottle pointed to me and the bottom to Harry Felter. Once was enough. He kissed me on the cheek (doesn't even know how to kiss). He is beginning to grow a beard. I think it will stay soft and fuzzy for a long time. I liked the way it felt when he turned his face away so quickly after he kissed me. It embarrassed him.

I'll be fourteen on Thanksgiving. Harry's friend

"Hi" Rabinowitz calls me a turkey. He also called me a gilded stinkweed. I don't know why he did. I hate him, although I used to have a crush on him. He's smart in history and wants to be a politician. Dick Feffer is smart in history too and wants to do something with it. Milton Sasslofsky is crazy about music. He whistles symphonies all the time and imitates bird calls. His instrument is the oboe. The first time I heard him play I made a fool out of myself by giggling; it sounded like snake music. Harry Felter (that genius) wants to be a doctor. His fingers must be strong enough from pounding that piano every day—strong enough to keep his patients down while he tortures them. He is helping a real doctor at Montefiore hospital with research on cancer in plants. Two days ago my ball rolled down the back of Montefiore hospital (I went there because maybe Harry would come out). There was a red light on the door and it said "MORGUE" in big black letters. I was afraid to go in (naturally). Harry's been in a number of times, he says. He likes to describe the way the corpses are filed away in long drawers, and how even though it's so cold in there, the drawers glide in and out easily because they're lubricated with graphite. He has a detailed mind, and come to think of it, it reminds me of the morgue, the way everything is hidden and nothing touches and he doesn't touch me.

That's what bothers me. He's a cold fish.

So you see, everyone I know does something intellectual. I wonder if that's why they act so old and at times unfriendly. Diana and Juanita (I'll get to her later) and Harry have been playing piano so long I feel stupid having to plow through my beginner's exercises. I want to play pieces with feeling. I like to do anything emotional, that's the way I am.

I like to make believe I come from a foreign country. In the bus coming home from school, Diana and I pretend we are speaking a foreign language. It makes me feel important to have command of words that no one else understands (not even me). Someone speaking in another tongue sounds somehow so much more intelligent than someone using the mother tongue. And what if Mother really put a fork in my tongue the way Aunt Bella suggested (violently)? Would I then have a forked tongue?

In the train I like to watch my image in the window. It's a dark image and hides my pimples. I think to myself, "That's how beautiful I'd look if I didn't have pimples." Sometimes I promise God to not wear make-up if he'd only give me a pretty complexion. But I don't believe in God, so it's no wonder my complexion stays bad.

Tuesday is a boring day: it isn't the first day of the week and it isn't the last day, it isn't the middle of the week, either, it just fills in. It's a lousy day because there's still three more days of school before the weekend. Last weekend I went to a party at a boy's house I don't know. Harry and Diana know him. He lives in a private house with a terrace. His name is Alfred; his friends call him Alfie. I think he liked me, but I didn't like him. Anyway, I was glad he liked me, because so few boys do. Diana danced ballet in the middle of the floor. All the boys looked at her. They always did. She has so much training. It makes her furious when she's not the center of attention. When she gets nervous she licks her lips and stubs her toes into the carpet as if she were packing lamb's wool into the tip of her toe shoes. She sits with her skirt above her knees and her lap spread wide, the same way she rests at the ballet studio after hard work. It's part of her show-off act. She gets the attention, all right! And I have to pretend I don't notice, because I'm second fiddle and bow and scrape. I don't know why she's my best friend.

I wish I knew. She doesn't act like a best friend. She went to Juanita's party without objecting, even though she knew Juanita didn't invite me on purpose because Juanita likes Harry too.

Juanita is a great big horse, but Harry likes her better than he likes me.

Brown leaves and coolness, great! I can wear my new velvet suit. Maybe it is "gilding the stinkweed," as Hi would say, but who deserves the transformation more? You can't miss me in the color red. I bought the suit to wear for a choral performance. The sopranos stand in the back, so all anyone will be able to see of me is my face. Mother says she'd be able to see and hear me even if I was a thousand miles away. Pretty good trick—but the usual type of mother magic. Oh my poor old mother. She's thirty-three already. I hope I don't look like that when I grow up. How can I avoid it?

Cousin Lenny got a pinball machine for his birthday. It's a great big one and he keeps it under his bed. It rings bells, and the balls that roll into the holes are made of lead. He wouldn't let me play with it, but when he went down, I did. It's a boring game that you can play by yourself. After a while the score doesn't mean a thing: it always adds up to more than 25,000. At first it excited me and it seemed a lot. Millionaires must feel that way about their money; they lose sense of what it means. That's why they leave such big tips.

No homework for the weekend. That is, no written homework. I have to practice that stupid song "Hark, Hark, the Lark," and also one I like, "*Voi Che Sapete.*" Whatever I sing, my teeth seem to stick together like magnets and the chords stick out in my throat. I'm not very relaxed. I don't have the natural flow that born singers have. The teacher told me to quiver my lower jaw like a rabbit's nose, imagine I was throwing my voice upward and outward, hold my belly in, put one foot forward, smile when I sing *ee*, roll my *rrr*'s, etc. During practice we have to pull our tongues out of our mouths with a hanky so they won't slip back. Singing is pretty phony, if you ask me—not an expression of anything human. Maybe that's the way to be great: do all the awful things anyone else would rather die than do.

I'm not going to do anything today. I'm miserable. My parents had another one of their dirty, cursing fights and my father told my mother to go to hell. When I went in to stop them I was shouted at too. Mother threatened to beat me up for interrupting. I locked myself in the bathroom and contemplated poisoning myself. I put a glass on the window sill and poured iodine, clorox, cough medicine, soap, etc., into it. I was feeling so bad I was about to drink it, but the more stuff I added, the more interested I became in the color changes. Finally the whole mess turned a slimy gray and I poured it out the window. It was too disgusting. Dawn came up the same color as the poison.

Called for Darlene in her house, Hunter Hall. She has a stall shower. I saw her undressed and was surprised. She has breasts as long as my grandmother's. I couldn't take my eyes off them. She wasn't embarrassed, either. At least she has lovely hair (it's short and curly like a Greek god's), and she has a rosy complexion.

We met Janice on the benches. She wears thick lenses in her glasses. Her eyes are brown and wet and shaky. She has kinky hair and thick ankles. I wish I had a pair of brown loafers like she has. She gets anything she wants. I don't particularly like Janice or Darlene; they're drips.

Diana's ballet master calls her "lemon" because she wears a yellow leotard and tutu. He calls all the dancers by the color of their outfit. He bangs on the floor with a cane. Diana and Anyi Lynkopf are his best pupils. I noticed that when a male dancer picked Anyi up during an adagio his hand rested on her crotch and he had a way of running his hands over her body. Anyi seldom smiles, because her teeth are very bad; rotting green and pointed.

The dressing room smells like Sweat Cologne. The dancers douse themselves with it. They wash their feet in the sink.

Sunday I went to the annual performance of Sordkin pupils. Diana was in *Coppélia.* I sat on the top tier of collapsible benches that were placed against the wall of the rehearsal studio. Diana played the doll in the shop window who comes to life. After the performance she ran past me gleaming with sweat. It's hard work coming to life. I thought when she was dressed she would draw me into her circle of friends and we'd all go for a hot chocolate or something, but she ignored me and I didn't want to force myself on her.

I told my mother not to tell and she goes telling everyone. Yes, I'm ashamed that I got a piano scholarship. I got it by crying, by pretending I was so broken up because I couldn't play well. Boy can I cry, what self-pity! I don't really give a damn about the piano.

My teacher is a Bach expert and what a stickler for perfection. She has a real adversary in me; I manage to play things well with my right hand, but the left bumbles along like a dead nerve. I can't possibly remember what key a piece begins in, and have no way of playing it by heart; flats go sharp and naturals run rampant, eighth notes are held for four counts while I grope for the next series of dotted eighths and sixteenths. My teacher cries out in her German accent; "Why do you sabotage me?" She shoves me off the bench with her thick body and proceeds to flash through an invention.

It was cold when I came for my fifth lesson, and she made me sit on my hands to warm them up. They were still numb when I dashed through my scales, and she slapped them with a ruler and insulted me. I don't like her attitude. Just because I don't pay, she wants to whip me into a genius; well, I don't genius that easily.

six

Grandma G. loves me and I love her, but when Aunt Bella (she feels better) took us all to the Jewish theater last week and I asked Grandma for a cherry life-saver in the car, she wouldn't give it to me. She hides sour-balls, cherry life-savers, and hard raspberries in a secret zippered compartment in her handbag. I wonder why she acts so selfish? All of a sudden candy is the only thing in her life.

Grisha the Communist has a large yellow pad that he writes on. I wish I had it. I admire him because he once had something published in a newspaper. He lost his job because of it and they black-balled him in the industry. I think he was an operator on dresses and an organizer. Uncle Grisha reads a lot. He wants to give me a bunch of pamphlets and books on theories he believes in. Mother says his wife made him suffer; that she left him for another man. Well, that sort of thing is bound to hurt, but I thought Communists were used to switching around. I always forget that everyone is human. Aunt Bella made Lila cry. Lila is Grisha's daughter. Bella insulted her mother. Maybe striking out at other people makes Aunt Bella feel in the swing of things. To be alive is to attack. Although to be alive is also to fall down.

Uncle Ernie lives with Grandma G. She has a bed in the living room and he has the bedroom by himself. I like to dwell on how Ernie is, because I don't like him. He's stupid and secret. He is very thin with a pot belly (looks like a case of native malnutrition), belches a lot out of his turtle face, greases his hair, and uses Craig toothpaste. Whatever he uses he smells half fresh and half oily (dirty hair and clean teeth). He always gets to the toilet first. This is his thing. Grandma G. says he sits so long because at work they have bad toilets. He smokes continually in the toilet and creates a heavy smoke screen.

Grandma believes very much in the enema. She used to clean her kids out the minute they got sick. Ernie's enemas must have made some impression on him: he has a stake in that territory.

He never holds a conversation. He says hello and goodbye; in between he works, eats, and sleeps. He has what Mother calls a cigarette cough; it sounds like when someone tries to start a motor boat. Ernie is Mom's kid brother. His face is hairless. He reminds me of a cured midget. He lends Dad money to get out of debt. Dad is in perpetual debt the way others are in perpetual adoration or mourning—debt becomes him, it gives him his attitude. He is the mad debtor. Doesn't deny himself anything, though. People are always signing for him and regretting it. He has charm. It's a charm that people who don't care about anything have. Sometimes I think he'd just as soon drop dead as go on living. He makes jokes about it. He has no responsibility. Why does he go on working? Maybe he likes to have a good time even though he complains, and maybe he complains to us to keep us away from his money. Yet I always can get movie money from him. What he says is: "You shouldn't ever go downtown with less than three dollars in your pocket."

Ernie is a sucker for Dad. Dad uses his handball, money, and signature on loans: for this, Ernie gets free suppositories.

Mother tells me to be nice to Ernie, because sometimes we "eat off him." The family is forever trying to marry him off and no one suits him. Grandma doesn't want him left without a caretaker when she dies (can't she see he's sexless?). It's pitiful the way the whole family goes through the farce with him. They even pack his bag for him when he goes to Laurel-in-the-Pines. He comes back tan but unengaged. The relatives suspect there's something wrong, but say he's still young and he'll get married when the right girl comes along. Mother says he has a good heart. Save me from men who have good hearts!

Ernie is a member of the "clean-plate club": whatever Grandma puts on his plate he eats. She throws the food on as if she was aiming three pounds of whipped butter at a cockroach. He eats and then the belches bubble out of his bubble pipe. In our family I'm so aware of everyone's insides. They never let you forget it. It's like in some families they make you listen to sonny's violin or sister's piano. Ernie is a master of the belch. He belches and it's treated with reverence.

On the other hand, his rival is Uncle Ben, who has a specialty of his own. He buys the most expensive handkerchiefs, and then makes a show of how big they are and how soft the material and how hand-rolled the edge and how curly the initial in the corner. He never uses the handkerchief to blow his nose; instead he sits picking it with an aristocratic pinky. He knows it disgusts me, so he hoists it aloft. Then he slowly inserts the finger in the handkerchief and wipes it off; then he folds it carefully and puts it back in his jacket pocket; then he says, "Hello, Rosie O'Grady" as if he just saw me and he changes my name as if it were a joke.

I learned something funny about Communists: they may seem serious and know-it-all, but underneath they're sentimental and prone to believe the impossible. Now, Uncle Grisha naturally thinks his brother Ernie is a creep: Ernie reads comics and colors in coloring books. But when Orson Welles produced the Martians are coming gag, Grisha got so scared that he took Grandma G. and Ernie and ran into the street and kept running. That's an example of what mother preaches: "Blood is thicker than water."

Blood: The Drink You Eat With a Spoon.

:

I was going to Grandma G's to play rummy with her, but Mother met me on the street and told me she had just died.

Outside her door there was a straw mummy case. The door was open. Inside, two men were talking to Aunt Ray. Nobody was in the living room. I started to go in. Aunt Ray stopped me. "You can't go in there." I could see that the room was sunny. Ray and Mom went into the kitchen. I sneaked into the living room.

Grandma lay under a brand-new sheet. It was so sharply folded and crisp that it gave me the impression I could shape a boat or a plane out of it like a Japanese paper toy. I thought, "This is her transportation." I wanted to whisper, "Where to?" because I believe dead people hear you but can't let you know they do. So I got closer and called her "sweetheart" and "dear," and patted her hair.

Her skin was blotchy and there was cheese in the corners of her eyes. Her hands were crossed at her breast but there wasn't anything in them; I saw her glasses on the night table and put them on her chest (half funny, half serious), I'm-laughing-with-tears-in-my-eyes kind of thing. I really wanted her to take them with her, because who knows.

All the windows were closed. Why do people shut off the air supply so fast? The room was a preview of the tomb.

Mother finally noticed I wasn't with her and rushed in to drag me out. "You're a mean kid, you know Grandma wouldn't have wanted you to see her that way. Couldn't you have waited for the viewing?" Grandma a monument? If so, I should have crept under the cover with her to be revealed at the unveiling like Charlie Chaplin in the arms of a statue.

I sat on the steps outside till they took Grandma G. to the museum and I stood over her while the men made room in the van. I thought all the human things about her I could, because if she hadn't been born and given birth to my mother, I wouldn't have been born. I thought about how she had to go to the toilet once when I was there and peed in her pants because she didn't have bladder control. I thought of how she had grabbed my breasts suddenly one afternoon when I was about to go to the Tuxedo matinee, and said, "You've got a handful, you'll be okay." I thought it was a vulgar thing for her to do then, but now it strikes me as affectionate and the grandma kind of thing to do.

Went to the funeral. Walked slow and didn't smile. Felt like smiling. My mother in fat black, Blanche in medium black, and Bella in skinny black with a touch of dropsy black. It was a lovely sunny day. I kept thinking, "I'm alive." Completely removed from the tragedy of it. Maybe I'm always removed; it's better to remove yourself before someone does it for you. A romantic idea (the way I really am): I'd go home and find Grandma sitting on the Majestic radio where her picture used to be. I'd ask her to move over just a little so that I could reach the dials. We'd listen to *The Yiddishe Philosopher* together as a courtesy on my part, because I'd really want to hear *Little Orphan Annie* and test my code ring.

Think of something you don't want to happen or something you don't want to own and presto it's yours and it comes to live with you. Ernie is ours. He took my room and I have the piano room. I can see the reservoir and De Witt Clinton High School from my windows. Ernie came in at night and tried to see something through his toy telescope. I hate him. Mother treats him like her child. It's enough that I have to put up with my sister—the only place I can ignore her for the most part is on these pages. Mother forces Ernie to eat. She washes his underwear. He doesn't talk to me. Yesterday he gave sister a Hershey bar. He likes little kids: they don't pass judgment on him. He's a big tease: first he says to her, "You want it?" and then when she reaches for it, he sits on it and makes her try to get it. I think it's disgusting; the chocolate must be body temperature by the time she gets it. Then he plays ball with her and sooner or later it hits her between the legs. All his games are for him!

Only one of Ernie's drawers has clothes in it; the rest of his bureau is filled with junk. He keeps his underwear in the top drawer. Next drawer down has: lighter fluid and two Ronson lighters, a carton of Camels, a photo album, two pairs of glasses, and assorted Hershey bars. The drawer smells terrible. Third drawer down: a coloring set, a paint set, a Hohner harmonica, a deck of pinochle cards, and a wrench. Bottom drawer: radio parts and tools. That was it: not a Trojan in the whole mess. What a private life.

:

Today Mother admitted to me that there might be something a little off in Ernie, but to humor him because Grandma would have wanted it that way. Nobody caters to me. I suppose if I was the village idiot I'd get fantastic treatment.

I am the village idiot, but everyone else is, too. We wear peaked caps, and carry eggs home in them. On the way we suck the yolks out. At night we drink shell soup and sing egg songs. We play hide-and-seek among the hills. Some of us get lost forever, but most of us carry on the tradition.

seven

At last I'm able to sit here without being afraid. Nobody is in the house but me. The rest of the family went to the movies to see Andy Hardy. I had locked myself in the toilet because I heard noises. Our apartment is very big. I waited for the noises to stop. I imagined someone sneaking around with murder in his heart. I didn't like being confined, because there wasn't anything to do in there. Finally I got brave (cowards do) and called out, "Come and get me, I'm ready for you!" I half knew it was only the wind rattling the panes or a shade flapping outside the window. Mother has to have all the windows open, even in cold weather. She fears that we'll wake up dead some morning because of a gas leak. She examines the pilot light to see if it's still on; let God be your pilot and the flame will burn bright. There are wonderful things in my house; both idols and idlers are viewed suspiciously.

My hair is still wet. The last time I washed it, Arty watched me while I played the young enchantress. I brushed my hair as voluptuously as I could, stroking and patting and letting it fan out electrically. I pretended that he was my lover and I was tantalizing him. I turned gracefully so that he could get every angle clearly in his mind. Why was I doing this to Arty? Because Arty doesn't like girls and it was safe to practice on him. Many's the time I kissed and petted with him on the benches in vain. He is revolting, he spits when he talks. His mother likes me because I'm his only girl-friend. They don't mind sacrificing someone else's child.

Went to a party tonight at Diana's. Met a new boy whose name is Elliot. Diana turned the lights out and we were stuck with each other. He asked me—and these are his exact words—"May I caress your charms?" I had to push him off because they weren't my charms, they were my falsies. Now Elliot thinks I'm a prude. He's a smooth operator; what I mean is, he acts and talks polite, but underneath he wants to do something dirty.

My lips were awfully swollen from kissing. Why do boys think that the harder they kiss, the better it will be? Maybe it's because they're boys. What I like is the suspense (a build-up): breathing on my neck, a hand up and down my back, rubbing against my breasts so that I wonder what's happening next. Will he or won't he? I covered my entire face with calamine lotion so that my parents wouldn't notice my swollen lips.

Tomorrow I get my period, just when I was planning to go to the St. George pool. I really could go swimming, I don't believe in that old-fashioned stuff, but the water would run red from between my legs and that's embarrassing. Instead I think I'll go to the Tuxedo and soak up a little darkness and entertainment. Maybe Diana'll go with me.

A LIST OF MY FAVORITES

COLOR: BLUE—IT LOOKS WELL ON ME

FOOD: CHOPPED HERRING AND EGGPLANT ON WHITE BREAD WITH TOMATO

CLOTHES: SPORT—BECAUSE I'M SUCH A SPORT (HAH!)
GAME: TENNIS—SOMETIMES I'M THE RACQUET, SOMETIMES THE BALL
MOVIE: *The Good Earth*—SAD CHINESE PICTURE
ACTOR: CARY GRANT—I DON'T KNOW ANYONE LIKE HIM
ACTRESS: DEANNA DURBIN—I WISH I WAS HER
MOTHER: MINE—SOMEONE ELSE'S MIGHT BE WORSE
FATHER: DIANA'S—HE'S SO HANDSOME AND CONTROLLED
SUBJECT: ENGLISH—BECAUSE I'M INTERESTED IN READING AND WRITING
HOUR: DUSK—BECAUSE IT'S MYSTERIOUS
FRIEND: DIANA—BECAUSE I LOVE HER
BOY-FRIEND: HARRY—BUT HE DOESN'T KNOW IT
SONG: "MOONLIGHT SERENADE," "I STAND AT YOUR GATE," ETC.
DANCE: THE LINDY—LOVE THAT RHYTHM
HOBBY: LISTENING—I LIKE TO HEAR WHAT PEOPLE ARE SAYING
AMBITION: FOR HARRY TO TAKE ME OUT—AND TO BE GREAT SOMEHOW

The steam just went on. It dries me up. I wish I was in England where the weather's damp and complexions bloom. Our teacher pointed out that England is a land of eccentrics. That's where I belong. I do strange things. For instance I dress up in costumes and dance on the roof. Don't I know what to do with myself? It's my primitive rite in the sun. I embrace the elements. The direct rays hit me, go through me. Nothing else goes through me. I hold on to the pipes that are on the roof and do leg kicks and squats. Sometimes I wrap my legs around a pipe and lean way back; I tighten my stomach muscles and come up in one tight piece. I don't know why I exercise so much, I just like to. I'm thinking of going on a diet. Why don't I get into shape? I can have a good body and look like a dancer. I mean I can be as thin as Diana. Brave talk! I'm so weak-willed when it comes to eating; what will ever take its place?

Harry has a sex quiz he wants to try on some of Diana's friends. I wonder what it asks? Diana says that Harry met a girl at Loon Lake who taught him the facts of life. It's hard to believe. I would have liked to do that, but I don't have the facts at my fingertips. Someday I'm going to make love to him if I don't move away.

Diana showed me a very funny thing. It's called *How To Run a Car*. She got it from Arty. It's really *How to Make Love*. I wonder what Arty is interested in that for. He's a fag, although general knowledge is useful to anyone. Who knows, he may change someday in the far and distant future. You'd never know he was a fag unless you started noticing little things like his manicured nails and the swishy way he dances, as if he were endlessly involved in a solo featuring the pear-shaped ass and the revolving navel. He asks you to dance, and the minute you do he's off in the middle of the floor leering and extending his hand like a chiffon hanky to the other boys in the room. They tolerate it because he's their friend. We all like him even though he's queer, because he has good ideas and is the life of the party. I feel sorry for Arty's mother. She thinks he has lots of girls. He does, if you care to translate boys into girls; that's his language.

How To Run a Car

First grease all parts carefully. See that her points are lubricated and fit properly. Look into her motor and make sure that it's clean and in running order. Now get into the driver's seat. Adjust it. Put your key into her ignition and get her going. Hear that motor purr. Step down on the gas a little harder, make her roar. Keep it up till she's ready to go. Remember to signal that you're about to go, then steer her gently and carefully away from the curb. Accelerate the motor. Look around and go! When you're on the road give her all you've got if she's seasoned. You're on your way to learning how to drive a car. That is if you remembered to shift gears and go into three positions.

When the going is tough use the first; when your speed is up use the second; and when there's clear sailing ahead and you're going full speed take her into third. Driving takes a lot out of you, but anyone can learn if they apply themselves and get a good car. The right owner can get years and years of service out of an old car. A properly cared-for car can be traded in at the right time and the whole thing repeated again and again—so long and happy motoring!

eight

I wish I didn't have to deal with parents. Just put the money in an envelope and send it to me care of the Riviera.

Mom claims that Murray the vegetable man likes her and picks out the best for her. Yesterday we received soft, moldy strawberries. The ones on top were okay but the fillers leaked a bitter red wine.

So much for Murray in his dirty white apron using his position of trust to pawn off rotting fruit. He has no integrity, just doesn't care whether he keeps us as customers. Mother "trusts" too often and doesn't pay her bills. That's why storekeepers don't respect her. She orders by phone as if she were asking favors in fear: "You have good bananas today? Maybe you could pick me out some nice soup greens? I don't mind if you throw in a cantaloupe if you smell a ripe one."

Out to the benches again with my records. Diana brought her portable record player. We wore sheer peasant blouses. I'm thicker (the real peasant). She has a round face, I have round arms, she has strong calfs, I have strong thighs, her waist is tiny, mine is broad. I'm the work horse, she's the aristocrat.

It wasn't fun on the benches tonight, no boys around. They must have been playing basketball. Games seem stupid to me. All that fuss and energy just to toss a ball through a ring. It would make some sense if you could throw yourself through the ring: rising, skimming the hoop, and then falling straight down through it, not stopping, going through the floor, the foundation, the earth. Every player lost because of the conditions of the game. We were disappointed but it wasn't the end of the world.

Wow, was I sad and bad and mad! I slashed the outside of my hands with a razor. I made deep criss-crosses in the flesh. A rehearsal for self-destruction? There wasn't much blood because the lines were so fine. I scarred my hands. It was easy to do because it didn't hurt. Even my brain was numb. Afterwards I bought pancake make-up to cover the cuts.

A young man I know would be scared away if he knew what I did. It's a strain being with him anyway. He's in the lingerie business. He lives with his parents and uses the apartment to take girls to when they're away summers in the Borscht Belt. He's jealous of me playing the piano. I hate dabblers like Larry. He's twenty-eight and is just taking piano for the first time. His real talent lies in conning mothers. My mother is crazy about him. He brought her flowers and me perfume. He looks like a Teddy bear, and even wears woolly brown double-breasted suits.

My hands are healing. I canceled my piano lesson. Mr. Jalisco my new teacher would be horrified. He's a nervous wreck by nature, plays the fast pieces faster than necessary.

I wish I could get help. Someone who would listen and say, "Insanity is not imminent." I already know that insanity is not peppermint; it is green pistachio—my favorite ice cream; I ask for it, but they seldom have it.

I can't bear going shopping with my mother. She has patience with those stupid clods of sales people. God, they drag out stuff that doesn't suit me at all. She makes me try it on anyway: "How do you know it looks bad if you don't give it a chance?" She knows and I know that a wide-hipped, short-waisted girl cannot wear long waists and gathered skirts. She tortures me.

"But I hate it," I tell her. She whispers that I'll insult the clerk. Then I insult the clerk on purpose: "Don't bother helping me, I can find what I want by myself." The sales person snoops around and shoves her ugly head through the curtains of the booth while I'm undressing: "Are you okay?" My body in its torn underwear is not for her to see, the clean-corseted frump! "I'll let you know later," I answer her, making my expression as ominous as possible. I can see myself from every angle in those dressing-room mirrors. Why does Mother insist that I'm beautiful? Is she blind or cruel? Doesn't she know that I'm deformed? Yes deformed! Deformed like a poor bastard hunchback, only in front, under the breasts where the line should be flat and long (not bulky and bony). When I was examined for camp the doctors called it Harrison's groove. I wonder who else has it? I want to hide. I hate myself.

nine

Today is Friday. I'm supposed to go out tonight with Larry. He has tickets for *Carmen.* It seems that whenever I go to the opera I see *Carmen.* I never see anything else. I'd like to see *Aida.* I've heard so much about it—how real camels walk across the stage. I have a blue dress with stripes down the side to make me look taller, and a new matching straw hat and new high heels. Mother used up her food money for my outfit. She did it for Larry's benefit, not mine.

Same evening after *Carmen:* I cried. She didn't deserve to die. It was her nature to drive men mad. Some men are weak and can't take it. Larry bought a box of cherries and orange drinks during intermission. He smiles all the time. It means nothing. Is he hiding something or is it a social grace? He's the oldest man I've ever gone out with, and I'm not sure how to act. I feel like being stupid around him and doing silly things to disturb his manners.

Larry isn't all manners. He's a dirty businessman. We went for a drive and he stopped the car and pushed me down and got his hand caught in my skirt zipper. I told him to cut it out or I'd tell his mother on him. He just kept on repeating in a very breathy way, "Let me fuck you, baby, let me fuck you, please let me fuck you." He rolled around on top of me. I was disgusted; he creased my new dress, he scratched my face, he made my foot fall asleep. Mother thinks he wants to marry me. She'd get rid of me at the drop of a hat. He had no right to talk like that to me. I never gave him cause. I don't even like him. He's used to older girls.

:

Mother says it's my fault Larry doesn't come to see us (get the *us*) any more, and wants to know what I did to insult him. I got mad and told her I had accused him of wearing the ladies' underwear he manufactures. This appealed to her vulgar nature and instead of making a mean face she burst out laughing. It shocked me. What kind of mother is she, anyway?

I saw Larry getting on the bus to Fordham Road, so I got off. My face was full of pimples. The pimples were covered with calamine lotion. What a sight! I should have stayed on and sat down next to him and made him gaze at me in my bumpy, chalk-pink mask and then begged him in falsetto, "Fuck me, please fuck me, fuck me now and forever, fuck me on the seat, fuck me under the seat, fuck my frozen landscaped face." That would have taught him disbelief. He'd be the one to have to leave the bus and I'd shout after him, "I am driven by desperation."

Uncle Grisha asked me why I'm not good to my mother. She complains about me to the relatives.

Says I'm mean and ungrateful. They detest me. Sometimes she boasts about me and compares me to their own dull offspring. This does not make them admire me.

I've stopped playing piano. I enjoyed it but couldn't learn anything competently except Chopin's Étude in A. I'd try to be playing it whenever I expected a date. I wouldn't stop playing till he was directly behind me; then and only then did I rise to greet him. It was a romantic notion I had. Oh to be admired and loved! I don't think anyone will ever love me. I have nothing to offer.

I have a friend Netty who's very nutty. She was one of the girls I met at Camp Bronx House. Her skin is pearly and her breasts stand up. Just a lovely-looking girl. If you want to know why I say she's very nutty, I can't; my lips are sealed. Here's a hint: she likes girls.

I finally met Netty's brother. He's very smart, a French major. We went for a walk in the cold. The benches had snow on them but we sat down. Hank put his arm around me. I didn't even feel it, I was wearing so much clothing. He tried to kiss me. His breath is awful, the worst I've smelled yet.

If it wasn't for his breath I might have kissed him. He pulled a dirty trick on me. He put his hand up my dress before I knew what was happening. I had a wild sensation, something I couldn't hold back. It reminded me of when I was eight years old and woke up that way from a dream. I like it very much. I hope it happens again soon. It's the fatal way I might go—so warm and good from beginning to end.

I've seen my whole family running around without clothes on. So what! It's natural. My father's penis hangs down in front like an unpressed tie.

I almost defiled Mother's brand-new bedspreads. Saturday she came home with two beautiful plaid chintz spreads. I had decided to have intercourse with Hank because I knew him. Well, we went into the bedroom and I took my clothes off and lay on the bed, on the new spread. Hank took his things off too. He has a long torso and short legs like an Oriental. He stood by the closet, and as he walked toward me an untoward thing happened: he kind of doubled up and jerked in and out like a South American dance. "Was that an orgasm?" I asked (my new word for the week). He grinned in a painful way. "I can't control myself, sorry," he said. Then we heard the front door being opened. Hank dressed faster than he ever had in his life. What a close call!

Mother asked Hank how he was and he said, "Fine." It amuses me the way people never know anything about anyone else, especially the sex that goes on.

Hank's mother is a horror. She's jealous of me. She won't let me use Hank's typewriter when I'm over there. Says I'll break it. The fat fool. My mother is more generous. With my mother, other people come first.

Hank's brother is religious and you know what that means: bigoted, compulsive, fanatic, and insane. He refuses to take advantage of modern times. He's twice as pompous as Hank. At least Netty's fun. I really enjoyed her company the Sunday we read *All's Well That Ends Well*, under a tree in Van Cortlandt.

I'm tired of pretending I believe in God to Hank. He's getting as religious as his brother. Says his wife will have to shave off all her hair, and that means pubic, under-arm, and head. Is it possible to buy a pubic wig? What if it slips? I'm also tired of reading the *Post* editorials just so that he and I can have intelligent, liberal discussions. Wouldn't it be more natural to just bore each other, which we really do, except when we're feeling each other up behind De Witt Clinton High School? Another thing about Hank, he doesn't want to do *that* as much as I do and begs off just when I'm getting hot. So much for that, and trying to do the mysterious and loving thing.

ten

When I was thirteen, Mother took me to see my second cousin Marshall Baxter. He felt me up while I sat next to him on a love seat in his hotel suite. I didn't know what to do, so I didn't do anything. Mother wanted me to sing for him, to persuade him to get me a screen test. Marshall was a well-known Hollywood comedian, but he certainly wasn't going to thrust me into the lap of fame. What I want to say is that I think Marshall Baxter is a kind of sex maniac, because whenever I went to see him after that he unzipped his fly. I rather liked the whole thing—seeing someone famous in their true setting. Marshall was after IT all the time. He invited me to visit him backstage last year when he was in a Broadway musical. I saw him in his dressing room. He was seated in front of a mirror surrounded by light bulbs. His wrinkles were full of pancake make-up. He was lounging around in a paisley satin robe. He drew me onto his lap. "You like it, don't you?" he asked. I thought he meant the excitement of being backstage, and I did enjoy that, but his hand went down between the satin edges of his robe. And there it was again. "You've got a winner there," I said. "You can be a winner too," he answered. I laughed as he good-naturedly went back to perfecting his make-up. I saw part of the show and practically puked, it was so boring. He kept eating bananas and throwing the skins away while he played the piano. He ate at least twenty bananas. Some act! He's far from original. I wonder if his daughter knows what her father is like.

To continue the adventures of Me: picture me in a new pink cotton dress walking down the carpeted hotel corridor of the Hotel Warwick. I am going to see that old and licentious man about town, Marshall Baxter. He is in his room with two companions, one a millionaire and the other a dress manufacturer. Marshall's night table is crowded with medicine bottles. Marshall calls room service for drinks. The millionaire (who is a synthetic rubber baron) and the dress manufacturer go down to the cocktail lounge to wait for us. The drinks come. We drink and talk —my aspirations: college, dance, drama. He listens while he toys with my tits. What can I say to this man, he's from another world. He wants to know what I do with my boy-friends. He thinks I'm sex on wheels. I tell him "that's private." "You can tell me," he whispers and goes to his knees, kissing my panties under the dress. I pull away and leave him kissing the air. He thinks I'm playing him for a sucker. "C'mere," he shouts, and twists my arm. This time he means business. He opens his fly and orders, "Kiss it!" He is meaner than his penis. It looks relatively sober. I feel affection for it and do as he orders. Then we go out and have a swell time at the Copa where everyone knows him (even the lady who tells fortunes there; he says she's a whore on the side). We sit at a reserved table.

Marshall talked about me to the synthetic rubber baron, who invited me to his office on 34th Street. He told me about his Washington affiliations and how great he was to have invented phony rubber soles to help the war effort. He opened his crummy scrapbooks for me to see his face on every page. The minute the work day was over and his staff left—oo la la! He dragged me within inches of his peculiar and dangerous mustache. Each end of it was as stiff and pointed as a leather punching tool. I asked him how he got his mustache to stay so neat. He opened his desk drawer and handed me a tiny round box of imported pomade. He put the stuff on his mustache, drawing it out thinner and thinner. I was very disinterested. On a table, he had arranged a display of shoes he had produced soles for, but there weren't any pairs. I had thought maybe I could take home a pair.

We sat down on the couch and kissed. Then he told me a story about how some foreigner was having intercourse with his sweetheart but he didn't move at all and kept it in a whole week till he came. "That is the greatest sexual thing that can happen to anyone," he said. I thought he was crazy. Then he asked me, "Do you wear a brassiere?" I told him I didn't need to and he seemed pleased. He leaned back on the leather cushions and slowly pulled a Baxter trick. He exposed himself. "I hear you're the best in the business," he said. It was the first time anyone ever told me I was best at anything, so I worked extra hard and invented a new technique. It dealt with the off-beat. I had to synchronize what I was doing to the beating of his heart; very much like improvising a counter-point to Bach.

Tell me I'm good at dying and I'll do it.

The Baron lent me his car and chauffeur to go see a play. He told me there'd be tickets waiting at the box office. It was a thrill. I felt as if I was powerful and rich. I don't think I'll ever be rich, not like those people. Baron (I call him that because he's so famous he has to remain anonymous) gave me fifty dollars to buy something to wear.

The let-down of the year came in Baron's penthouse. We were served venison from one of his estates. That was fine. The valet leaned over me with a silver tray covered with choice cubes of the steak. That was great. I was too dumb to know that I serve myself, so the Baron put some meat on my plate. I ate my meat without changing the fork hand to hand; you can eat faster that way and I think it's an approved method. Well, then I was primed for a super-special dessert. Dessert is my favorite course, but what a dud it turned out to be. The valet brought out a plate of chocolate Oreos.

The Baron's penthouse is like a house. There is a wide staircase leading to the second floor. Between the first and second landing he has a huge painting. I asked him who painted it and he got mad. He told me that in polite society one never asks such questions. He said it would be different if I asked him how big it was. I thought his concern about size was strange; I go for quality. Then I put my foot in it again by saying what a nice polite elevator man he had. He said, "You talked to the elevator man! My dear, don't ever do that again."

The elevator opens right smack in the penthouse foyer. It's a private elevator. The Baron's study, which he never uses, is decorated like a monk's, and in his living room he keeps part of the original Gates of Gethsemane (whatever that is).

I don't hardly remember what we did in bed, probably 69, but it ended up 11 (side by side we won't collide). His bathroom is splendid. He keeps two gallon bottles of Macy's mouthwash under the sink and four toothbrushes hanging from a golden eagle on the wall. The toilet looks like a white wicker chair, and if you forget to raise the seat, you get strained pee. The shower has eight nozzles jutting out of the wall for different parts of the body. It can be adjusted for fine or coarse spray. I took a long shower and used a transparent soap with no odor at all. Afterwards I tried his colognes. One, imported from Jamaica, smelled like limes. His talc was flesh-tinted; I powdered the inside of my thighs. My mouth had a terrible alcohol taste because I had licked it off the Baron's scrupulously clean body. I used the mouthwash and it burned my gums.

When I came down to the living room the Baron was impatient. He handed me fifty dollars. I had been planning to ask him for an educational loan (college fantasy again). In the shower I had been daydreaming about how I would arrive at school in his chauffeured car and pretend he was my father. He's at least fifty-five and I'm fifteen. I don't think I'll see him any more. He's not my path to glory.

Diana goes on and on, cool as a cucumber. She doesn't have to do anything bad to get what she wants. My secret life is all bad and yet . . . She says she wants to marry a man who is not smart or talented so that he will cater to her. I want to marry a man who is brilliant so that it will rub off on me. I can't tell if I'm dumb or just uneducated. Lately all I'm trying to do is prove I'm attractive to men. Dad thinks Diana is beautiful. What does he think I am, a turnip? When I have gatherings, he dances with her.

eleven

My paternal grandfather is a big man with nose trouble. We've all inherited his nose. I don't think my father's nose is his own. It's part of my grandfather's, which was extremely large. Even though it's large he can't breathe through it. Nobody else can, either. I have a deviated septum. Only one side at a time works. Dad tries blowing out very hard and then breathes in fast to try to catch the air when the nose isn't looking, so to speak. Sometimes I hold my arms up in the air to breathe better. It's too bad that's the only thing that's free is air, because it causes such a daily struggle.

Grandpa may not be able to breathe through his nose but he talks through it. The only one he talks to is Father, and their conversation sounds like a snort contest. How they love each other and hate my mother. Grandma hates Mother too. They must hate me because I'm the daughter of my mother. Let me tell you how disgusting people can be—evil in small ways, so that it piles up.

Our furniture is falling apart and Grandma and Grandpa have a second-hand store. Grandma promised Mom a chair and a lamp and a cocktail table. We went to pick the stuff out. Dad was waiting for us at the store. He shouted at her that he wouldn't allow any junk into the house. She screamed back at him that he never bought her anything new. He hit her. He forced her arms behind her back. Grandpa shined a flashlight into her eyes to make her stop screaming. I kicked Dad and knocked the flashlight out of Grandpa's hand. I hate that old bastard. Mother and I ran out of the store crying. We were on Third Avenue and 102nd Street. Mother said, "Stop crying, the colored people will think something's wrong." What did she mean by that?

:

Grandma (my father's mother) invited us to dinner last night. She makes awful food: calf's-foot jelly with garlic, herring with boiled potatoes, and tea with lemon. She berated Mother for the umpteenth time about how her son could have been a doctor if it wasn't for Mom rushing him into marriage. Dad tells them everything about Mother. He even calls her crazy—his own wife. He has no shame. They laugh at her behind her back. I'm very cold to those people. When Grandpa takes out his violin (he taught himself to play) and plays, and everyone says I got my musical talent from him, I deny it.

Grandma took me into the bedroom to show me a new bathrobe Dad got her for her ancient birthday. She stripped off her undershirt (she wears a man's undershirt) to show me her breasts. "Just like a girl," she boasted. Her skin is strange—like a coal miner's. The pores are large like orange peel (especially around the breasts), and there is dirt in them. Her face is the same, and her hands are always gray. She washes, but because of the kind of work she does in the store she can't ever get clean. She's different than Grandma Gold was: tough and wiry, delivers furniture in a pushcart without help from anyone. She's proud of that.

I love to explore her bedroom. There are

treasures there. In metal boxes pushed under the bed she keeps diamond tie-pins, rings, bracelets, earrings, and other shiny beautiful objects like amber umbrella handles and ivory cane heads. Mother says she buys stolen goods. She once sold Marshall Baxter's wife a chinchilla jacket for fifteen dollars. She didn't know its value. Marshall Baxter's mother is Grandma's sister. I knew her when I was little and everyone called her "Tante."

I wondered why Grandma suddenly became so nice to Mother. Now I know; she thinks she's going to die. Dad found her out cold in the bathroom yesterday. The toilet bowl was full of blood. Maybe she will die. I couldn't care less. Poor Dad, he hates hospitals so much and now his mother is in one. Maybe I'm a cold fish, but I'd like to see all my enemies get it.

I stay up nights worrying about death. You can run anywhere and it follows you, it follows so close that I wonder how can death be so quick? Death is in us already, that's how. Death is the great love of my life; once is enough.

:

Everyone is passing. Last night, in his sleep, Grandpa went, soundproof after all that noisy breathing. Now the house is haunted. Grandpa had a stroke—no more Grandpa-ville.

Goodbye, Grandpop. If you sneeze you might blow your way out of hell. If you fart (and I know dead people do) you may zoom your gas-propelled way heavenward.

Expected news! Grandpop left me nothing in his will.

Think I'll go see Aunt Ray. She has a new dog. His name is Sandy. She's the only one in the family who allows an animal in the house. That doesn't make her great—it kind of softens the mean things she does. I'm not afraid of Sandy even though he barks. Once a dog sicked me and I froze. My fingertips got tight and I couldn't move from the spot. That saved me.

I can't stop eating. I gorge myself on candy and cake and soda. I can't help it. I get these overwhelming urges to eat. Eating is my surrender to satisfaction. It is the answer to "I want." And I want plenty. Food is mine to grow hungry for, and consume. It's always fun to decide what to eat. Appetite is the one rule, and appetite is what I have. I am hungry, always hungry, and this puts me in a class with lovers and artists—I have no other choice.

twelve

Aunt Bella is extremely ill again. Friends and Uncle Mort's business associates have surrounded her with goodies, dried fruit, candy, smoked oysters, giant fruit from Florida, and imported biscuits from England. Now, what could be more idiotic? Bella is being fed intravenously.

The nurse is a real cock-tease, waving her ass in front of Uncle Mort (with Aunt Bella on her death bed in the other room)! She threw a whole pack of cards on the rug and then bent down to pick them up slowly, one by one. She was demonstrating a ligament-stretching exercise. "Bend from the waist," she explained, "to get the most benefit from this exercise."

One day last week when Mom and I went to see Bella, before she had her relapse, we found her in the kitchen, sitting on a high stool, making fruit jello for Uncle Mort. She was too tired to get back into bed by herself. Imagine, just to cook for her husband, to do the wifely thing. I suppose I'll hang on to life that way too; by doing normal things as if they were normal for me.

I'll never know what Aunt Bella wanted when she motioned me to come closer. She was lying on a bed with wheels, her dropsical stomach high under the sheet. Her shrunken yellow face and long thin fingers frightened me. I thought she would dig in and not let go. She smiled; I backed up to make room for the wild animal. Oh, I'm so bad, so guilty; Aunt Bella was the only one in the family who read books.

If I dream about Aunt Bella she'll live again,
but more briefly than before.

:

I'd hate being old and decrepit. I couldn't stand it if it took me an hour to get a cup of lukewarm tea to my mouth and the only other thing I was allowed to eat was boiled rice. I hate being slow because I'm quick. Old people are probably reassured by their own pantomime: "If it takes me five minutes to get two steps from the table to the chair, how long will it take me to go from life to death? At the rate I'm going, maybe never."

Slept at Uncle Mort's apartment last night. Why? Because I was too tired to go all the way home from downtown. I did have some ideas about WIDOWED HUSBAND AND YOUNG GIRL, but put away the evil thought. I can just see the headlines:

UNCE AVUNCULAR SEDUCES NICE NIECE

The girl's mother found the pair involved intimately on the living-room floor when she entered with a passkey to remove some of her deceased sister's belongings. The uncle, known as Uncle Mort, is being detained presently at the 15th precinct, where he is being held on charges of disturbing the morals of a minor. The girl was released in the custody of her mother.

Mort has fine Italian marble lamps. The ones by the bed have red bulbs in them. The glow made my skin look unblemished. When Mort came out of the toilet I went in and it was another kind of light entirely—fluorescent. I sprouted blue pimples. Uncle Mort smells like the Baron and wears real silk pajamas. He likes subdued colors like wine and blue. I was wearing a blue sheer nightgown but I did a crazy thing. When I was in the bathroom I took a roll of adhesive tape and wound it around my middle to nip in my waist and accent my breasts. Anything for attention, even if I didn't feel sexy. Uncle Mort said, "If you weren't such a tub of lard, I could get you a job modeling." He's finished in my book. Wait till I'm gorgeous and he has incestuous thoughts.

Brought A. home from school with me today. He's an Arabian fairy. We like each other. Drank milk and ate dates. Walked through a flat grassy place (a field?) in Van Cortlandt Park. The sun and sky above were in the right place and so were we. He's like a woman; we discussed make-up. His lips are cinnamon brown; I'll bet his penis is too. I can't help being attracted to him, even though I know I don't excite him. He's so elegant. I suppose the dirtier your mind is, the cleaner you'll try to be in person. Part of a famous quote which

I don't remember is: "Desire has pitched its tent, in the place of excrement." That's it, he wants to look furthest from his desire. I love his velvet vest. He has a Van Dyke beard and his nails are manicured. I feel like a mother to him. Protecting someone makes me feel protected. Mom is prejudiced but he'll win her over with his manners, and if he doesn't . . .

thirteen

Dad left early to open the drugstore. I had breakfast with Mom and little sis. Ernie is a late sleeper. We had poached eggs, toast, and coffee. Sister had four eggs and four pieces of toast. She's fatter than the Taj Mahal. Mother ate with her mouth open. I caught myself eating like an animal with chin in plate and tongue lapping away. Mom told me to straighten up. Dad never eats anything but a slice of whole-wheat toast and a wheat-germ capsule with his coffee. The meal was going along as expected when the phone rang and that disrupted everything. Mom got upset. She spoke in a secret way over the phone so that even I couldn't piece the conversation together. She turned to me and put me in charge of the toaster and clean-up because she had to run. It must have been important, because she did the black bottom in front of the mirror (shake your hips, slap your can) and put on her best girdle. She dances when she's excited, that's the childish part of her. I asked her where she was going and she told me to mind my own business.

Mom back at six, with a roast chicken in a silver bag. She looked sad. I'd like to know what she's up to these days. I mean she's very naive and impressionable. She's the one SPECIAL OFFERS attract. She's a sucker for the sweepstakes, trips to Bermuda, dance lessons, encyclopedias, and freezer units. God knows what she's doing to improve her lot in life.

She confessed to me because she had to: Mom has a detective trailing Dad. She thinks he has another family somewhere. Yesterday when the phone rang it was the detective with a big break-through in the case. He gave Mom the woman's phone number. Mom called the woman's husband and he gave her short shrift, but, the woman got wind of it and called Dad immediately. He choked up with rage and threatened to kill Mom. (I don't think he'll do it.) He said he's going to have the phone removed. Mom wants me to watch the phone in case someone comes to take it away. What he did is unscrew the earpiece and remove a wire, so we can't hear a thing on it. Without the phone Mom's lost. It's her social life and the way we get our food.

Mother's in the bath with the water steaming hot. Dad's got her pregnant again for spite. He won't bring home ergot to start her period. I'm afraid she'll faint in the tub and get rid of herself first. She's determined to abort. As far as I'm concerned, it's murder. I detest the idea. What if she hadn't wanted me?

It happened "naturally" as she was standing by the stove stirring chocolate pudding. Mom held it up for me to see: a plastic bag of water about as big as a golf ball. "See, it's nothing," she said, and it slipped from her hands and split open on the bathroom floor. She bled for a week while pieces of the placenta appeared every day. No pain, no nothing! Just thick chunks of the placenta floating folded in a bottle of alcohol. She would shake the bottle up and say, "That's the nourishment." Her vulgar and unfeeling attitude toward nature confused me. I could understand the primitive fear of the afterbirth, the burying of it, even the isolation of a menstruating female, that I had read about in a Margaret Mead book, but I wasn't prepared for her complete lack of superstition or guilt, or for her "scientific" discoveries. If the doctor hadn't appropriated the specimen in order to determine whether all of it had come out and nothing was left to cause hemorrhaging, she might have kept it on her knick-knack shelf as a conversation piece.

I miss the child that never was
I miss the child that used to be
I miss myself right now
Where am I?

fourteen

ATTENTION: the time is now. It always was and will be. What shall I not do? I shall not do my math homework. I shall make small decisions that are in opposition to the existing order of things. Neither math, nor history, nor musical theory can ever again expect me to rehash the theories that make them possible. I'm screwing up.

Mrs. Plover asked me to conduct the Beethoven *Fifth;* she got sore at me because I wanted to do the whole symphony and kept swinging the baton in an insanely enthusiastic way. She wanted to divide the movements among others in the class. I had a great time with Toscanini backing me up. The physical labor wrung me out. Mrs. Plover leaned over me (upswept like her hairdo) and warned me: "You're not passing this term, either. You refuse to obey instructions, your homework is less than perfect, your behavior in class is disruptive to others who are serious about their work." She forgot to add: "and I hate your adolescent female guts!" She couldn't hate them more than I do.

I like to watch that sex-mad theory teacher operate. She wears pointy brassieres under low-cut, tight-fitting, knee-length dresses (often knitted and hugging her butt). She's been married twice that I know of. All during class she bends over our theory notebooks correcting, which gives her an opportunity to show what she's got. We all joke about it, but it's quite a disruptive display from someone who abhors disruptives.

Diana is winning top honors, kudos, and the admiration of all her teachers. Nothing can bring her down. I think our differences are contained in the essentials. For instance, I glanced down at my legs during official class and noticed that my stockings were sagging and had runs in them. She was neat as a pin. She respects herself. Every layer of her from bare bones to underwear to trim velvet suit is a framework so devoid of clutter, so balanced, that it can be built upon, and supported. I was already collapsing from the inside out; my clothes showed it. I allowed my hair to grow very long (mid-back), and when I wanted to hide, I made an effective screen by fluffing it forward on each side. My head became a hot hairy nest of bluebirds (of happiness?) smothering each other. Follow the bluebird of happiness and it will send you crashing through impenetrable thickets. Diana just puts out her hand.

I'm failing. Geometry has me beat. Too many rules before I can find out: HOW BIG—DISTANCE AROUND—SHORTEST WAY THROUGH? Why can't I just GO?

At times I amaze myself and others by knowing the answer. It works against me, because then "teach" thinks I can do better. She never lets up. She wants blood. They always want blood, and blood takes time, blood takes at least an hour every night of studying; the hour when I'd rather be doing something else, like eating or reading or creating soapy hair styles that defy gravity. I'd rather do worse (I'm a disappointment). When I lose interest, no threat in the world can bring it back.

French is completely foreign to me. Nice teacher, though. Her name is Madame Soupalt and she's married to a cello teacher, Mr. Tallow. She's cheery and good-natured, a joy to behold. She has no scapegoats and no favorites in class. I think she's interested in her personal life.

There should be one tense: the present. Other tenses are fantasies. I don't object to fantasies, I have a few myself, but I don't think fantasies should be made so difficult—fantasies should come easy and in your own language.

English! Now there's the subject I love. WORDS, WORDS, WORDS, WORDS. Now what does that WORD mean? Say it fast and repeat it often—it means nothing. It means I forgot what it means. It forgot what I mean. What they mean. Mean—they're mean—certainly mean! THE RATS —THE RATS—THE RATS WORDS SWORDS WARDS SWORDS WARDS WOINDS WOUNDS WOUNDS.

POEM

word rats
are wounded

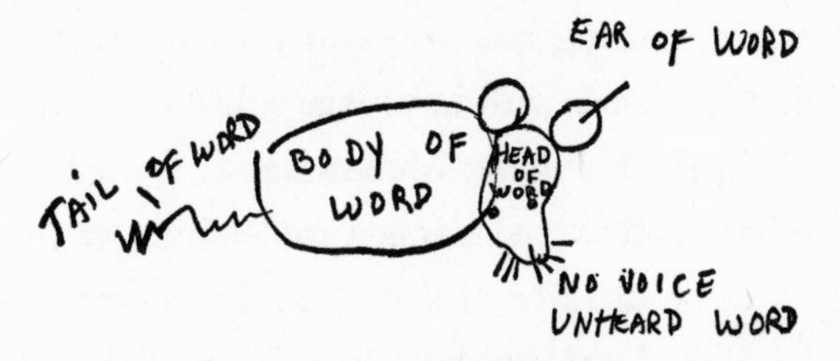

Yesterday in school our math teacher hypnotized some kids. I remembered how to do it. When fat Maria came down the steps after school, I asked her if she wanted to be hypnotized. She said, "Maybe." I promised to improve her flute playing if she let me experiment with her. She made me promise not to touch her silver flute, because it came apart in sections and only flute players could put it together again properly. I said, "Okay." I took her behind the back stairs that led from the gymnasium and started to talk to her in a very confidential monotonous voice. I did everything right except I almost forgot to tell her that when I clap my hands three times and tell her to wake up she should wake up. I made her write her name like she used to when she was seven years old; asked her to play a difficult piece without making mistakes (which she did, but it was dull as dishwater); asked her whether any boy had touched her; asked her whether her mother still slept with her father (she mumbled). I was bored with Maria because it seemed her parents never did anything outrageous to her or to each other, and her experience with boys was nil. Anyway, I was still in there playing Mandrake: I planted the idea in her head that she was a ravishing creature and had to be extra careful around the opposite sex, also that she would be a world-famous flutist within three years if she practiced four hours a day. When I brought her out of it she didn't believe I had hypnotized her until I showed her the piece of paper she had written her seven-year-old name on. I hardly believed it myself. I had all that power and didn't know what to do with it. It made me feel weak.

The most frightening question I can ask myself is: Where does time go? Something happens, but where is it stored? I mean, is all gesture, all energy lost? Will there ever be a real time machine like in *Alley Oop?* God, imagine doing over and over again the same things that were practically unendurable at first. What a refresher course the time machine would be: a baby born ten times; a casual affair extending beyond any permanent one; accidents screeching to abrupt but useless stops; my father calling, "So long, you old bag" to my mother as he runs down the stairs an infinity of times.

Dad wants to see what I'm been writing. Fat chance! One mention of birth, death, or copulation on the printed page and he tears it up. I should have another book going just for him. Hearts and flowers. If he became insistent, I could drag that out. It would be absolutely idyllic and have a trick ending.

fifteen

Nothing to do again. Friends away at Rockaway. Met that nut Nathan who thinks Beethoven speaks directly to him, gives him messages through the symphonies. Nathan plays the violin, hates me to call it a fiddle, calling a violin a fiddle Americanizes it, gets it ready for a career of square dances instead of Paganini. I like to get his goat, except that it's easy to bother a nut and a trifle dangerous. He's ugly, has a big nose, short body, and black oily hair—THEN WHY DID I SLEEP

WITH HIM? I have no morals sometimes. Maybe if the library was open on Sunday I would have been there instead of in Nathan's house, in his mother's bed. It was interesting but not intimate, because I was ashamed.

That Nathan came home from the navy and told me he had syph. I rushed over to Dr. Reiss and asked his advice. He acted like an old granny. Probably jealous. He said he'd have to report it if I had contracted the disease. Luckily the lab report gave me a clean bill of health. I wouldn't be surprised if Nathan got his venereal information from Beethoven too.

I bought a new brassiere. It's white satin; the cups make my breasts look like engorged bullet heads (one step closer and I fire). Nathan's brother was down by the benches and I wondered what he'd do if he saw me in my bra. I called him over and he was terribly flattered, because I go with the older crowd. I asked him to sit down and tell me how Nathan was doing in the navy. It got darker out, but there was plenty of light from the moon to make me visible. Joey looks like a baby ape; it amuses me. I let him put his head on my shoulder. His thick hair tickled my ear and neck. I lifted my blouse till it was above my collarbones. Joey looked. I asked him how he liked it, and he said he liked it fine. Then he asked, "Is that all you?" I made him touch me to prove it. My breasts are the most sensitive part of me. I get a thrill every time someone lays their hands on me. Isn't that an old cure-all, the "laying-on of hands?" Joey was so impressed he couldn't let go, kept adjusting my "treasures" as if they were a pair of out-of-focus binoculars. "Sighted the enemy yet?" I asked, as he gently brushed my nipples against his eyelids. "There's no one around," he whispered. "No enemies, and no friends." He was sounding too philosophical for me, and since I couldn't tell what he really meant, I broke the spell with: "Why is it that your whole family is so ugly?" And he countered with: "Nathan says you're a nymphomaniac." "To who does he say it?" I glared and punched him in the ribs. He grabbed both my arms and twisted them behind me. The baby ape was strong. "I don't know," he said, "just everybody he knows. He warned them about you." He had his face pretty close to mine, so I spit in it; there wasn't much spit, just enough to make him draw back, and in that moment I wrenched free and ran. So that's what they're saying about me. I wonder if Harry believes it? Truth is stranger than fiction, though; what if they knew about the Baron?

Stood in the library overwhelmed by titles: *Green Mansions*, *The Jungle Book*, *Droll Tales*, *Boswell's Journal*, *One Life One Kopek*, *Anna Karenina*, *The Moth and the Flame*, *Silas Marner*, *Penguin Island*, and *A Tale of Two Cities*. My eyes got stuck. I couldn't choose one. The librarian offered to help, but there was no helping me; I didn't want to read, I wanted to sense the overwhelming mystery of shelved creation.

I'd like my life to be as quiet as a library; and for each day to leave an indelible stamp on my mind, so that when I return (to that day), I will know for sure it's the right day. I think I'll be a writer; it just comes out of me.

Mother disgusted me today (again). I asked her how it felt to give birth and she said, "It's just like going to the toilet." How can she compare me to a turd! I suppose she didn't want to frighten me about pain and horror.

sixteen

Who knows what evil lurks in the hearts of men? Dr. Reiss dressed in his spotless lab coat makes me stand nude on a chair to get my sun-lamp treatments. I wear sunglasses. He's giving me the treatments free so I can get rid of my pimples. It's damned white of him. He kisses my legs and pats my behind. When I tell him I'm overweight he says I'm perfect. What kind of doctor is he, anyway? The least he could do is weigh me and tell me what to eat. The first time I went to his office I had a long wait, so I took a book of skin diseases out of his bookcase to read. I sat on the floor helpless with horror at all the ugly skins—finally I was comparing symptoms. I came to the conclusion that what I had was not acne but some obscure Mediterranean blotch. When Reiss came out to get me I was pretty depressed. His professional diagnosis cheered me up, though. He said, "And to prove you're not contagious, here's a little kiss." He kissed my cheek. I had a feeling he'd do something romantic—he's so old world.

Saw the beginning of an operation. I was sterile and stood right near the operating table. First they painted the patient's back with red stuff and put a needle in her spine. I started to black out when they sliced her belly and the blood popped out of the fatty tissue like tiny red berries. Nothing was visible except the excavation site. Her head was under a canopy and she couldn't see her body. She was talking to the anesthetist about her kids. Dr. Reiss was at the knife. He doesn't think I'm so tough any more. He was sore that I had to leave the operating room before his big scene: the skillful removal of three shimmering gallstones. I made it up to him at the next sun-lamp treatment—

drove him wild with desire. Now he wants to take me out for *Wiener Schnitzel* and Viennese coffee, a bill of fare I might not refuse. He said he'd like to be in charge of educating my palate.

Whenever I am guilty about anything, or after a bad fight, a spot on my outer right thigh about the size of a quarter gets hot. Why my upsetness should show itself to me in this way I have no idea. It's painted red in my mind like the "stop" button in the elevator, but it's not where anyone can reach it.

I'll never know some things, as long as I live.

We had a treat today after school. Elizabeth Schumann blasted out in the grandiose manner. (Music and Art is often visited by celebrities.) She stood on the stage where Mr. Cuneol usually conducts chorus IV, up in the tower. The size of her bosom helps her interpret German lieder. Everyone but me practically burst their Lifelines with applause. First of all I hate the doom sound of German, and here was this frau firmly stanced (one leg forward, one back, hands clasped below bosom) singing about trout and forests as if they were about to be destroyed. Most people laugh at classical music and they're right: it's for special people who want to be alone with their FEELINGS.

Charged up the hill again to get to school late. Sat in the "late" room thinking about my first doll carriage. It was enameled in wine color and had lovely satin dolly covers. Uncle Mort had given it to me for my Dydee doll. I used to make her drink bottle after bottle of warm water till the tepid fake pee-pee soaked through her diaper. Pee-pee makes it real. That doll was my baby. I still have her in the closet. Her cheeks are painted with nail polish, her belly is cracked, her hair is crayoned over, and the pissy leak hole has a broken toothpick stuck in it. I always like to put something into something—fill the empty spaces so the wind won't whistle through. Now who'll do the same for me?

Sometimes you hate people for things they can't help. I was walking down our dark hall very fast.

I thought I knew where the door was, but I smashed into it with my nose. It hurt like hell. I sat on the floor crying "Momma." I felt like a big doll—limp and lifeless except for the squeak box inside. I'm ashamed of the warmth that comes over me when my mother is kind, yet I really can't stand her. And I repeat: it isn't her fault that she disturbs me. For instance, Daddy, Mommy and I are walking along the edge of the park to get to the bus stop near Jerome Avenue. We are on our way to Loew's Paradise to have a good time. Daddy insists that I walk with him and shoves Mother ahead to walk by herself. "You look nice enough to be my girl-friend," he says to me. My mother turns around for a moment to smile at me, and he hisses, "Keep going, you old bag." He thinks of himself as young, handsome, and irresistible. He wants to disassociate himself from the middle-aged, thick-heeled, eye-glassed woman in front of him. I ask him to walk with her. He refuses. I refuse to walk with him, and so we approach the bus stop separate, Indian file, strangers to all appearances.

STRANGERS

A play in the Dark

1ST STRANGER: Suddenly it has become dark.
2ND STRANGER: No, gradually it became dark.
3RD STRANGER: It has always been dark.

DAYDREAMS BY ME

I walk into the library and Harry Felter is there at the science section. He looks up and doesn't smile or say hello to me, so I go to him swiftly and say, "Ah, Harry, have I ever kissed you?" And then I kiss him soft and sweet on the mouth and leave him alone again.

I am lying on the grass in Van Cortlandt Park, right near the golf course. Someone says, "Use your mashie," and Harry settles right on top of me, mashes me to the ground. "I'm not a sled, Harry," I tell him, too warm to move. And he says, "I'm not a belly wop, Selma; I'm a Jew on your back."

I visit the Felter home. Diana is leaning against her Knabe concert grand. The fringe of a red and gold paisley cloth . . . ? Elegant arpeggios. She whispers, "You again, what do you want?"

"Let me take you away from all this."

I avert my eyes for an instant and see that her foot has changed into a brass pedal. She can only hide one at a time.

"Well, then," I say (superior), "I suppose you intend to sustain one chord for the rest of your life."

Her mother enters with a can of metal polish.

MOTHER AS CLEOPATRA: It's cooler on the water. The water is breaking my heart. I could die.

FATHER AS POTENTATE: Get those slave girls some nice tailored suits.

The Baron is in touch with me again. He wants to introduce me to his boy-friend (tonight at eight at his place). He asked me to wear a veil and long white kid gloves. Why did he specify? I'll send him the bill. No skin off my ass. Maybe it's a fancy party.

It was a fancy party. Very fancy, with blowers and noisemakers, and feathered hats, and tootsie rolls, and chocolate kisses, and candles, and whipped-cream cake: blowers, noisemakers, hats, ostrich plumes, tootsie rolls, chocolate, kisses, candles, whipped cream cake: blowmakers, feathered tootsies, candle rolls, fancy kisses, and chocolate very. During which with candles and whipped cream I rolled like an ostrich kissing the cake and plumed from behind. Lots of things I never did before, or was ever asked to. The Baron and his friend Jack had written their requests down on a cocktail napkin. It was pink and had a frolicking lamb.

"You'll like the attention you get," the Baron said, "if you've never been with two men before."

"Yeah," I said, "but it has to be dark."

"You don't lay the rules down, darling; we do," Jack said.

"Put this on."

He ordered me into a satin rag with no back and rhinestones hanging loosely fringelike around the neck. It was green. I hate green because it's life and death. Maybe I love green because it's life and death. Maybe I mentioned it before. I have simple ideas about color, like if I wear blue, it's a piece of sky; white, I'm invisible; brown, I fell into a pile of shit. And so on. They put green on me and I had my choice: sprout leaves or get pungent. I was as stale and packaged as those Oreos the Baron once offered me for dessert. "Watch me crumble," I thought, "for money." Together we can go places. I don't remember if I was present when it took place. I detached my retinal inter-view (closed my eyes, I mean), and watched from a great distance. It came to me that you can do anything as long as it's not you and you refuse to recognize yourself in the street.

I chewed and swallowed a dollar bill. It didn't taste like grass. Now I'm made of money but I don't grow on trees.

:

I'm saving the money the Baron gives me so that I can run away. When I have enough I'll just take off and forget the past. I have seventy-five dollars in my own account.

Nobody would guess what a stimulator I am. I wear very prudish clothes, but I am constantly preparing activities (in my mind) to spur men on. The more I excite their emptiness, the better I'll get paid, and I enjoy myself too.

seventeen

Aunt Ray has lent me a green velvet dress with leg-o'-mutton sleeves to wear tonight. I'm singing with the senior chorus because they don't have enough sopranos. Mother says Aunt Ray is selfish because she doesn't invite Mother to play mah-jongg with her friends. Why doesn't Mother have her own friends?

Mah-jongg has a great sound. I drop the ivories on each other just to hear them click: bam, crack, flower! Arranging them on the racks reminds me of my button game. It's a solitary race; I line up red buttons on one side of a box cover, and black on the other. Then I say to myself, "I'm the red (or the black)." I slant the cover and the buttons slide down. If my color reaches bottom first, I win. What do I win? I don't know—maybe luck. I keep playing. Usually I'm comfortably in bed—tired, warm, mindless—when I take out the button box. The reason we have so many buttons is Daddy used to sell them. He didn't stay in the button and costume jewelry business long, because when everyone else was buying Czechoslovakian rhinestones, he said, "Who needs them." And then they made fortunes during the shortage and he was out in the cold. This is typical, but it isn't the family bad-luck story—we have a worse one, it goes like this: "We would have been millionaires today *if!*" It seems Dad had an opportunity to own a piece of Rexall drugstores but he turned it down. Maybe no one asked him. He's always failing what he tries; but Mom doesn't try at all.

I think of street names literally. For instance, Aunt Ray's street, Gates Place—not a gate in sight, just another Bronx block open at both ends. The newest house on the block has cockroaches, too. I know, because we were considering an apartment there, whatever that has to do with anything. I think I mean crummy things never advertise themselves, they just show up. Cockroaches have free passage so they just go, and where they go is your house. I hate it when they get into your drawers and nothing is clean.

Being clean keeps the secret that we stink.

Now I'm really mad. My maps are all over the floor of my room. Mom tore them off the walls. She said it was my room but she didn't mean it. It's her house, her everything. All I get is mean, rotten stupidities. There isn't even a lock on the door; everyone wanders in to rummage through my belongings.

What is she, this stay-at-home momma? I wish she'd stop patting me, kissing me on the lips, and pushing my hair off my face. And I can't stand the way she examines my panties before she washes them.

The time is not ripe for my mysterious exit. I have been digging into the x-checker for new clothes.

eighteen

Found a buggy kitten and fed it. Mother gave me a jar-top full of milk. Bye-bye, kitty, you can't come in.

Brought home a butterfly. Was allowed to keep this pet because it was dead. Set it in a box on top of cotton; tried to make it live by blowing on its wings and putting the box in the sun. It was permanently dead. I wanted to see how it was made and ripped the wings, squashed the body. Ugly green-black goo oozed out. Whoever may find me: DON'T DO THAT TO ME!

I also rip buds to make them bloom faster. I expect my brutality to cause a flourishing. This is because I pretend it's scientific. Any dismantling (flowers, crawling creatures, winged insects) comes under the heading of SCIENCE. I have a compulsion to pluck my eyebrows. I'm the victim of myself.

I've cut my hair off; I do that when I feel desperate. I could go into what hair means to me: strength (but Samson was a man), beauty, warmth (stuff my pillow), love. I've cut myself off from these things and I said out loud, "Damn it, off it goes." I couldn't stop cutting till it was very boyish. Now my head is light, is clean, is small and fine; shaped to the skull à la Jeanne d'Arc.

Saw a mysterious thing in science class today; a lima bean between layers of wet cotton sprouted a cotyledon (like an erect clitoris). First there was nothing visible; then its own nature drew it out into the damp warmth. The skin shriveled, was no longer needed. I thought of my own body.

At home I took a mirror and put it down between my legs much as a dentist examines the back of gums. This is what I saw: something like a mussel gone bad; narrow, fat-lipped, and reddish-brown. The urinary orifice was larger than expected and the mouth of the vagina slightly obstructed by inner flesh. The whole area seemed underdeveloped. I was really curious to know what men see when they look. I don't like it. It leaves me wide open.

I'm not jealous of Diana; I want to own her, I want to be necessary to her. We were both wearing red hair-bands today. I worry about her; she thinks her mother wants to poison her. She loves her father but is afraid of his temper. She sounds like me. I didn't know she was afraid of her parents. Live and learn. It surprised me when she wrote on our public school graduation picture: "To a sweet girl who is my dearest friend." (A message from the queen—her head was crowned with braids.) There is someone who is closer to her than I am, but this girl is completely ugly and hairy and weak and her name is Shirley. The only reason she is number one is because the families are close. My family is far.

I am so sick; my pajamas hurt my flesh, that's how I know I have fever. It's fun to write when you're sick, because the words seem to float. I have nothing else to do. I can't stand the sheets, my toes keep pushing against them. I smell toast toasting. Mother is making chicken soup. I hear things being done for ME. The doctor says I have the grippe and to rest away the illness. I love being sick.

I dreamt about trying to get out of school; I kept going up and down, and whenever I reached what I thought was an exit, the door was locked and I had to start all over again: go to the top, cross the halls, reach the principal's office, wait, walk through the office and down the steps again.

I have dreams about steps often, usually about the Third Avenue El. I go up the steps and then I'm crawling along unprotected girders; I almost fall.

I'm in the movies. I go to the balcony. I start to fall down the steps and I tell myself it's only a dream. Then I wake up.

I'm in a ship going to Europe. Suddenly I'm in a rowboat in the dark waters. I'm in the way of the big ship. Then I'm in the water.

I'm in California. I take a ferry. I'm in the water. Or I cross a bridge to get to the ferry to take me to a mountain top where I sit down. I never return. I wake up.

I'm clinging to the outside of a bell tower. It is snowing. There is a light shining through narrow windows of the bell tower. I reach the window and tear out the central portion of the window frame. I look in. The fall inside is as steep as the fall outside. I know that I am doomed and make no other efforts. I wake up.

I hate falling dreams; dreams where you try to run but can't; and dreams in toilets where before you know it men and women use the same toilets; and dreams where you swim in deep, steamy water indoors and almost drown.

I've been asked to leave school. Yesterday I cut gym, and when the messenger asked if anyone in my class knew where I was, Diana told. What a friend. She can't resist giving information to the enemy.

The charming but cruel dean was seated in her office blowing her nose and wiping her bulging thyroidal eyes when I came in. She tucked her damp hanky up a long sleeve of rust wool; then she let me have it. (The rest of the snot that was clogging her think power. A long stream of it dribbled off her lips.) "You're temporarily suspended," she said.

So what. I felt rotten, but still, so what! A person like myself can enjoy being temporarily suspended! (A lie.) I like the rhythm of being suspended. (A lie.) Up there where she wants to hang me, I'll swing long distances like Tarzan and get out of the whole ugly mess. (Maybe.) Well, I'll have to let my class go on without me, even if my picture is already in the yearbook. Under the picture it says, "She has a winning smile." The bitch got very personal; she said, "You'll never find a husband, my dear, if you don't go to college."

I got depressed. When I get depressed I either get chicken or crazy, or both. So I mumbled, "Yes, Mrs. Forkin. How do I get to do that if I'm being kicked out?"

And she offered me the use of the school next year, which I declined by slamming a record book down on her desk and shouting, "You're nothing but a frigid bitch!"

I ran down two hundred steps to the Eighth Avenue subway. And will never run up them again.

nineteen

Who loves me now that I hate the world? Only my rock can. Oh, I know it doesn't really, but I dug it up out of my old camp trunk and sat it on the window sill. "You look young," I told it. "You haven't aged a bit. Let me show you how it feels to be thrown around."

I hefted my rock from hand to hand feeling its weight, and then, I missed. The rock landed on my toe. Smashed it so that I got blood on my sock. (It still hurts me when I wear high heels.) I cried and carried on the way I should have in school. Tell me, Talisman, did you want me to cry? All the people who want me to cry are: Harry Felter, Diana Felter, Mother, Father, and Mrs. Forkin. Sister Lucille hates for me to cry, it makes her frantic. She's over-sensitive. She heard me storming around and came in and sat close to me. Wherever I went in the room, she followed, trying to caress my hand. I told her to get the hell out and stop following me around like a dog, and when she didn't I asked her, "You really want to sympathize? You want to be a saint?" Before she could moon over me again I dropped the rock on her toe. She ran out screaming, which is her style too. That'll teach her to be good. I don't want to be her big sister, or anyone's big anything. Or anything.

They're sending me to camp again. They don't know what to do with me. Mother started a "Send Selma to Camp" fund among the relatives. They are not generous givers, but Mom managed to scrape enough together. She'd like to give me the best. Her fondest daydream (and mine) is that a rich family will adopt me.

I'm not talking to Diana any more. It hurts me

more than the rock. Now Harry is lost to me too. The Baron called. He knows what he wants. If only all the people who are so sure of themselves would get confused, it would help me. I hate his desires. Imagine, he thought I could get a girl-friend for a double date. I'd throw up before and after. Besides, I don't have any girl-friends, and if I did they wouldn't go out with rich old men and disgust themselves. I want to kill myself again, but I won't again. Think of Charley Rogen; he never had a chance and yet he makes plans for the future. I've had every opportunity, but it seems to be my downfall.

The camp I'm going to is some kind of liberal union camp. It's cheap. Uncle Grisha suggested it. As penance for being kicked out of school I'm not going to allow myself to write. At least not till I come back. Last night Mother cried on the kitchen table. She made me a salami sandwich when I came in. She says that Dad doesn't tell her where he works now. She thinks she has his number, but when she calls he disguises his voice and sounds Italian. He's a torturer. She says he keeps another full set of clothing at another house.

:

I'm back from camp. That was short. What happened? I went that-a-way. Let's follow me. No, don't unless you're prepared. For what? Real romance. What was he like? Was he great? He was an actor.

He was seedy: bad teeth, falling hair, canvas shoes with taffy-colored rubber soles. Sexy, though. He had an aura. The first night in camp there was a dance in the casino. I waltzed for half an hour with a union organizer. While we were waltzing he plugged the health-giving qualities of carrot juice and honey. I danced as fast as I could, finally leading, hoping to throw him off, but he hung on. John (the actor) introduced himself after the dance as I was fanning my armpits and blowing cool air into them.

"You shouldn't do that," he said.

"Why not?" I asked.

"Because," he answered, "it's more fun if a man does it, like this."

"I never sweated so much," I said, embarrassed.

"You're a healthy young animal." He put his arm around me. "How would you like to go canoeing?"

"Um-hum," I said, so we went.

I fell out of the canoe.

"You'll drown with all those clothes on." He

undressed me while I treaded water, and threw the clothes into the canoe. Then he embraced me, also treading water, and asked, "Are you a virgin?"

"Sure," I told him.

He didn't believe me.

"Don't you believe me?" I asked.

He dove under and found out I was lying. His finger floated around in me. "Little girls shouldn't tell lies," he said.

"You don't know about athletes and bike riders," I said. "Girl athletes have ruptured hymens. Your finger doesn't prove anything."

"Okay, have it your way," he said, soul-kissing me.

"I do have it my way." I bit his lip.

"Sleep with me tonight?" He wrote it on my thigh with his penis. It felt like the nose of a porpoise which feels like the head of a penis.

"Uh-uh!" I said, shaking my head. "How about tomorrow at four."

"Tomorrow at four'll do it," he agreed.

Four o'clock on the dot I arrived and interrupted John's nap. The cot was nice and warm and sagged in the middle.

"Here, let me put a pillow under your ass," he said.

"You don't sound very romantic," I told him. "Don't talk to me that way."

"As you wish, madam. The vulgar vernacular shall never leave my lips again to offend your ears."

I giggled because all I could see was his bald head between my legs. It wasn't what I wanted; maybe you have to develop a taste for things like that (like for liver).

There was a small screened window over the bed. Sun streamed in. John said I reminded him of *April Morn;* he also said my vagina was smooth as velvet. He isn't very original. We spent nap times together from then on. Once his roommate and a girl shared the bed opposite us. I didn't look, but what a thing to do!

There was recorded music every afternoon. We could sit on the lawn and listen. Once we made love a little early and could hear the *Eroica* all the way down the hill near the tennis courts where John's cabin was. I remember trying to come by thinking how the music sounded when John and I were together. How sad, life drags on. I wasn't exactly an automaton; I was a spectator participant. I watched every move but wasn't moved. (It's called The Experimental Summer. What makes just doing something an experiment? Put this into that and what do you get: tonic of sperm, the sound *aargh*, and clenched toes?) What a sweetheart John made! He nearly popped a blood vessel when he found out I had used his hairbrush. He was meticulous about that, the slob.

Everyone thought John was a bastard to ruin a nice kid like me. He wasn't evil—that was his life and the way he lived it. I told them. Anyway, an unusual thing happened to me through that guy. The second week I was there we were in the casino for community sing. John told me that a lesbian friend of his was paying him a visit and he was going to try to help her break the habit. I didn't understand what he was saying. He meant for me to keep away from his cabin door because he was making out with someone else. I came knocking; he didn't open the door, so I lay down in the dirt and screamed and cried. I was drunk on a few beers. I'm a cheap drunk. I kept shouting that he had promised to marry me. (He had and he hadn't.) I wanted to make him more of a bastard than he really was. Then the door did open and this huge female in his bathrobe stood there and said, "Cut the crap, honey, if you want to come in, come on." I said I wouldn't unless John asked me. He sat on the cot picking his feet and didn't say a word. I had the feeling that if I went in they'd tear me apart between them like a herring.

I stood up, turned around, and went back quietly to my cabin.

Mother don't cry for me.

The day I left camp I ate breakfast with John at the staff table. He hid a present for me under the napkin. It was a carrot with match-stick legs, match-stick arms, and a match-stick penis. There was a paper sign hung on the gift; it said: "PENIS PETE AT YOUR SERVICE." I put it in the side compartment of my valise and just yesterday found it again shriveled up and brown with the match sticks poking through the wax-paper wrappings. My type of souvenir.

Charley Rogen died. Leila wrote me that he was in a car that got out of control. All this time I have been nursing the idea that we'd get together sometime; now it gives me goose pimples. So that's what he grew up to be, a teen-age corpse. He won't have to kick anyone in the ass to show he's tough any more. Dead men never lift a finger or a foot; if they did, the earth would rise up like a giant rotten pancake.

twenty

I never thought that when Uncle Mort took everyone in the family from New York to Virginia for Cousin Lenny's wedding that I would be an eyewitness to its consummation. Perhaps "consummation" is the wrong word, because to consume something is to incorporate it into your own system (and it ceases to exist in its original form). What I saw was more like a poor dealer trying to shuffle the cards into one another smoothly, but only succeeding in jamming their edges together.

It took about eight hours to get to Richmond. Mother almost didn't go. She didn't have anything to wear. Uncle Mort gave her money to doll herself up. She bought everything black to look thinner. In black there's a kind of invisible boundary. Her accessories were: a silver mesh bag, silver pumps, and a white sequinned bolero bordered with silver sequins. Scales of a flounder and sequins are the same thing. I pretended they were, in my mind, so that when I asked Mother before we left the house, "Mom, are you fin, fin, finished?" I got stuck on the word 'finished.'

We sat in the train and Uncle Mort gave Mother a Camel. (He wanted to give her a hump.) Pretty awful of me to involve her in a dirty thought, but, she took the cigarette and inhaled. Only she doesn't inhale, she blows the smoke right out; she thinks she looks sophisticated. Uncle Mort embraced her in his bumbling clumsy relative way. What he feels must be like a giant order of boned chicken wrapped in a wet sponge. Her eyes froth over when he does that and she gets a "black-bottom" gaiety.

Dad spent his time on the train acting affluent. Uncle Mort knows some big people and some of them were his guests on the train. How do you get to be a "big" person? They took up the whole car. I wasn't too happy; it was about my dress. Dad bought it with me. He let me buy what I wanted. It was a violet taffeta dress with tiers of taffeta flaring out below the waist; each tier was separated by a blue velvet ribbon going all around. It had puffed sleeves. Mom blew her stack when she saw it. "You look like a wop in that dress!" She was truly distressed. I told her not to be vulgar about other people's nationalities and that she should be glad I liked cheerful, festive things. She clapped both her cheeks and pinched them, moaning, "How could you let her do it!" Dad, with instant hate and being the weak son of a bitch he was, shouted, "Do what you want! Take the lousy piece of crap back!" I wonder why they keep rehearsing the same parts over and over again (they won't forget their parts). Anyway, I refused to give the dress up. It was mine and it matched my eyes. Crazy Selma, that's me, fighting my way through the fog, arriving at the top of a mountain with no place else to turn but then, miraculously, cartoon-style walking on air to the next mountain.

Lenny's bride was called Honey. I don't know if that was her real name, but she dripped it sticky sweet all over everyone with that Southern drawl. Honey was and still is tiny. The wedding photographer took a picture of her in a three-way mirror; three of her makes one of anyone else. Even though her mother is totally unimportant to me, the sight of her with her daughter was an ugly sight not to be forgotten too soon. Imagine a piece of clay squeezed by a kindergartener and called "Lady"; imagine a crust-colored face shaved of all its features including eyebrows and eyelashes but seeded surprisingly with a sparse brown mustache. That was her in lace, the "face." They stood carefully together, hips meeting and arms locked behind, for a mother-daughter dream sequence before the wedding. The photographer snapped them in a flash: "Surprise!" Candid shot. "Mind doing that again? Just to make sure." And one with the groom in between them separating a prairie dog from its mound and hole in the desert. Who is this man? Is he the human male groom who all alone in the desert (Richmond, Va.) got so hot he had to make it with a furry creature? Or not so furry, flat hair glossed over with Honey. "That's it, both smile at the groom." They have tiny sharp teeth and no lips. What did my darling cousin get into. He is happy. I remember that he was happy and he offered me a chocolate from a giant red heart (box). It was the five-pound size and melted in layers. I took one that was wrapped in gold paper. It didn't deserve a medal. Fruit and nuts! How I hate fruits and nuts; I expected a soft center: burning with sweetness and luscious. There must have been one in there somewhere. (I didn't find it: I couldn't decipher the chocolate-swirl language that topped each one.)

Honey said, "Lenny's told me all about you. Ah'm so glad ya'll could come." She stepped out of her zip-up dogskin for a moment and I got a glimpse of her shimmering white-bride qualities. I envied her. Lenny was so athletic and tan. He had an intimate tic in his right eye that drove me crazy. It gave him star potential in my heart. In my heart I knew he was right, for me. I tossed and turned inside where I couldn't fall off. She offered me another chocolate. "No thank you," I joked, "there'll be nothing left for the worms." She turned to put the box back on the bureau or chest of drawers, whatever they call one or the other, I never could tell, and I smelled Chanel #5. I smelled it once before in a department store where they give free sprays.

I don't want to describe the wedding; just look it up under TRADITIONAL MODERNE. It had a smooth rolling time sequence: entry and welcome to all, ceremony, miniature weenies in baked wrappings and other goodies, exit to room two, the ballroom the chandeliers the geneology of tables, the cake on the table on the top of the main of the two main characters who. The young wedded couple were represented by a safe-food-colors-painted young wedded couple out of hard icing on the top of the cake. Sure it's confusing! I love primitive courtship, the nipples-in-hands dance, the dance-yourself-into-a-hole dance, and the let-us-all-join-in dance of sex. Lenny and Honey held the knife together and cut in. Cake. Cake instead of take! And an embarrassed kiss to satisfy the admiring relatives. They really like each other, and he has another home with her parents besides his own home and his father's home and his homeland, America. America the beautiful!

Lenny and Uncle Mort and Mom and Dad and not Lucille (she was too young to come) cried when the singer sang "My Yiddishe Momma." We were thinking about how much Aunt Bella would have wanted to be here at her son's wedding. I looked at Lenny eating and drinking like a pig on the dais and I remembered that he used to throw Uncle Mort's shoes into the toilet and also that I was present when he ran crying from the park after some bigger boys had stripped him and beat him up calling him a "sissy." He rose and opened the ball with a graceful glide and a whirl around the room with Honey. We applauded. A few relatives had bitter feelings about where they were seated. I was sitting with the young crowd toward the back of the room. In the official photograph I look like a shrunken head hung below a painted candelabra dangling at a field of face flowers.

Things loosened up. Uncle Mort danced with me. My elbows got stiff because I had to hold my arms way up to meet his hands. Dancing with him was like carrying something too wide, too far. He kissed me at the end of the dance and I opened my mouth. It was an impulse. He put his tongue in it and slid it around.

"You don't have to brush my teeth," I said. He laughed and pinched my ass. I hate pinching. We went back to eat. After every dance the dancers returned to their tables to eat. Melon and ice cream was for dessert. I took a piece of ice from my melon cup and pushed it against Uncle Mort's neck. The ice fell down. He made me find it on the floor. There wasn't anything left of it but a dirty puddle. He went and got his own ice and jammed it down the front of my "wop" dress. I stood there red in the face wanting to kill him. Aunt Ray brought a distant fat cousin for me to dance with. We trotted out into the mob and then Dad cut in: "Mind if I dance with my own daughter, son?" He kept passing couples I didn't know, saying, "This is my daughter."

The party ended in a mess with the women arguing who should take the flowers home, and the men hiding bottles of liquor so the waiters wouldn't get them. Everyone was grabbing. I drank two glasses of Cutty Sark and felt mighty sick. Uncle Mort called me over seriously. And he told me seriously that seriously I would have to share Lenny and Honey's room because a business associate of his had decided to stay overnight unexpectedly and would have to use my room. "If I have to," I answered. "If they don't mind." "There are twin beds in the room," Uncle Mort told me, "and you can have one of 'em. You look pretty tired. Why don't you take this key and run up ahead of them."

I was just dozing off when my cousins arrived. They were drunk. I know they were drunk because they were very loud and kept saying "shhsh." Lenny came and stood over my bed to see if I was asleep. I played dead. I couldn't stop breathing, though. I tried to black out once by pressing the big veins on each side of my neck. (Or are they veins? What's an aorta?) Out of the almond of my eye I watched as they passed a votive object between them. Lenny carried it into the bathroom and hung it dangling like a dead bird on the shower pipe. Its nozzle had a running nose. Then he closed the bathroom door and took a leak. Niagara Falls. (It certainly falls.) Niagara is a lovely name for a girl child. For instance: "Come here, Niagara child, don't be afraid. I won't hurt you. I want to see how you're growing, Niagara. My, your little breasts are puffing out, Niagara, Nigerian nigger of the Nile." And then he violates her!

The bed they were in (not my lonely one) made a lot of noise. It was saying: "I work while the city sleeps." The event was disembodied; fluttering sheets pumped other ghosts full of ectoplasm. If there was any flesh, it was held most tenderly in the folds of warm nightwear. The whole setup was phony. I think they wanted me to wake up and observe them; then there'd be little cries of chagrin and little leaps for safety and cover while exposing themselves to me. But it went on its plodding way, the dull descent, until it shuddered to a stop. Becoming another white nun of solitude, I crossed myself in mock Cathcolic, fingered my beads of sweat, confessed confusion, and tried to sleep by practicing a sin that is not a sin in my religion. It isn't even mentioned except about men, and they're not supposed to spill their seed upon the ground. I'm safe, I don't spill, and if I did I wouldn't cry.

twenty-one

When you don't like men you become an artist. Some guy I hate came to the house this afternoon. He has a round red face and lives on Central Park West in the Eldorado. His name is Bert. I met his brother and I like his brother better than him. Anyway, he brought this painfully ugly monster to see me with evil intent. I can just hear him lying: "She'll do it for you." The dumb-ox was a butcher. His own mouth hung open as if he had lugged himself off a meat hook. I'm afraid of butchers. Why did they choose that bloody profession? So Bert appeared with this prize package (blue ribbon) and my heart sank. God, the way Mother rushed in to announce them as if they were President Roosevelt and Winston Churchill. I was in the bedroom painting my first picture. How dare they interrupt the artist at work! I marched in regally and said, "I'm sorry, but you'll have to go, I'm busy." Bert asked me what I was so busy about; he was reluctant to leave and scared me.

"I'm painting a picture," I told him.

The butcher nudged Bert with his elbow as if to say, "Let's get outta here." Then they did leave and I was very, very glad. Of course Mother wanted to know why the two nice boys left so fast. She is innocent and the innocent never protect anyone, and are relentlessly clobbered by fate themselves.

Mother got mad at me today. (Getting mad is a daily exercise; mad muscles make superior mads.) She banged my skull with a frying pan. It cut my scalp; the blood came off on my hand when I reached up to judge the damage. I touched and looked and cried and even tasted the blood. I went in the bathroom and painted my face with it. Indian circles around the eyes made my eyes safe. (Don't step into the circle.) Red worry lines in a V put me into deep thought. And with delicate dips of the pinky into the inkwell of my scalp I tapped gory tears down my cheeks. "This is what you've done to me, Mother, made me a living mask au jus natural." She sent me to Dr. Reiss and he told me to not get dirt in it. He wouldn't put any stitches in. I told him that Mother hates me. He doesn't believe it. Thinks I must have made her nervous. It's true I called her a fat bitch and she is. I dusted the whole damn house for her and what does she do but go over the route again by herself. She says I don't do it right. She expects me to go into corners and find dust mice. Now I can go to hell for movie money. If I ate and breathed dust the way she does I'd be a cloud.

Lucille is giving her friends apples. She enjoys giving things away. I'd like to give her away to Dr. Reiss, ruin her. He'd accept her apples and make apple sauce out of them in his sterilizer. I like to look at her she's so healthy. Only ten, but her breasts need a brassiere. I don't want her to look at me, though. She hangs in the bathroom asking me how to put on lipstick and why do I wear mascara? She asks me, "Why do you smile at yourself in the mirror?" I tell her because I forget what I look like to other people.

Strange things happen, if they don't happen they're not strange, but whether they happen or not, boy it's something to be ashamed about. I don't know what came over me, but I felt very sexy. I was in bed and Lucille was in her bed. I crept into her bed and felt her up. She moved around and I got cold feet. She smiled at me in a friendly way. She's much nicer than I am. With me though, she's trying to buy in. No matter what she does her status doesn't change; she's a second-class citizen because she was born second. I came first and they love me best, because when they had me they still loved each other.

Visually speaking, she's an East Indian: dark, dank, secretive. I look at her and I hear ankle bells or temple bells or sacred cow bells. She has eyes that hypnotize: big brown; breasts that appetize: big down. She's everything I'll never have on my body. My slow glands against her fast ones. But slow developers live longer.

:

Stared at undressed dummies from the bus window. Hoped to incorporate their perfection by thought wave into my own undeveloped shape. When I stare at women I'm comparing myself. Sometimes the comparison is favorable: I'm too human.

Mother says, Why shouldn't I love both my daughters the same, why shouldn't I love them both they're both mine, and I bothed them both from the same stomach, the same soup for each right up to the measuring line, measure it, one baked potato each, each for each and all for all, half a cup, whole cup, five spoonfuls and whole fulls, leg, a leg, two legs in two mouths, fruit salad one a pineapple two a grape three a cherry four a pear five a ripe banana and six sectioned grapefruit, eat, eat, don't leave, keep even, line up there in the fair is fair parade. Don't hit!

I keep walking through the rooms. They get bigger. They get louder. The floors teeter-totter. The unused living room is dark. A shock of light from between the Venetian blinds blinds me. The closet door handle pulls off unexpectedly and I tumble backwards. I've been drinking sacramental wine and now I'm ill. It was too sweet. Life is sweet; the life level must be checked at regular intervals so it doesn't get too sweet. I faint; my life level is up and won't come down.

I say I want to be understood, yet I understand no one. I don't want to. I'm not capable of it. Yet what is there to understand? Do I mean: "Anticipate my wishes and act on them immediately, or out you go"? Pretty one-sided affair. If someone enjoys my mind and can take me as I am, then I am his forever. What's forever? Maybe I should be put away as Mom threatens. I am forced to suffer guilt because of weaklings, yet they are the strong ones. Mother is strong because she keeps taking punishment. I dish it out. She asks for it. I spit on her, make the toilet dirty, stay away from home, insult her accent, insult the way she eats (she sucks meat that gets stuck in her teeth, sounds like a bird call), make her carry packages up five flights of stairs alone. It makes her happy. She thrives.

Her whine turns my stomach. Why should I bear the burden of her life when I have none of my own? I wish I could get married. Maybe it wouldn't be so awful. Time to stop.

:

I am sick today: a cold. Can't breathe. Can think. Was thinking, why am I afraid to succeed, to finish what I start? Picture of long ago: I was ten. It was evening and I was in bed. Mom and Dad were entertaining in the living room. I heard him tell some jokes and laughed so hard I peed in bed. Mother changed the sheets and gave me new pajamas. I lay awake still laughing. Dad came in and told me a story about a kid who was piggish. This kid put pepper in two out of three pies, the unpeppered pie was for the kid, only he forgot which one it was and ate a terrible peppered pie by mistake. The moral was, I suppose, that wrongdoers are punished and what you do to others will be done to you. In my innocence I devised a ruse to stay up. I meticulously copied a picture out of a storybook and brought it into the living room pretending it was original. Dad accused me of being a liar. He insulted me in front of everyone. The more he insisted I was a liar, the more adamant I became about the origin of the picture. "Well," he ordered, "if you did it, do it again in front of all of us." I managed to produce a reasonable facsimile, which surprised him. I drew well out of stubbornness and fear. Then he said, "I just wanted to teach you a lesson, never lie!" Since then, even if I'm not lying I feel guilty, expect to be unmasked as a fraud.

Have decided that Dad tells stories with a moral because he's telling them to himself. He loves the gimmick. A story isn't worth its salt unless it's gimmicked up. I recall his favorite plot again: five people are on a plane, or ten people are on a train, the transportation crashes, strangers all, they are brought together by disaster (therein lies the crux of the flux), everyone's life unfolds systematically. How he'd love to outline his own life, put it into cliche order. But there's no rise and fall, no drama to his life. At least he doesn't think so. I've saved—no I found in the closet—his school notebooks. He studied botany and drew (because it was required) delicate studies of flowers and herbs. It could be the notebook of Leonardo da Vinci. I love my father but I'll never know him. Knowledge is a dangerous thing.

twenty-two

My goldfish died. All three. I kept them on the radiator and then the landlord got generous and gave us steam. The water practically boiled. By such remote and sudden decisions, fish near and dear to us often suffer catastrophe. Threw the fish into the toilet. One wouldn't go down. A pretty floating reminder—so reddish-gold in so coolish-green. It looked alive; the water was fanning its tail.

:

I was sitting on the sill of my open window looking out at the reservoir. It makes Mom nervous. She thinks I'll go into a faint and fall out, or throw myself out, or lose my balance and fall out. Why doesn't she push me out? She made me close the window. She was no sun lover. Ah wonderful sun, I was bathed in it, I was stretched in it like a big lace curtain on a frame. I'm an odd curtain. Mother can't find my other half. I don't worry; it'll turn up in someone else's laundry. Someone's millionaire laundry (wrapped around a cashmere argyll sock and a pair of silk shorts).

Mother is a contest fiend. The only thing she ever won was a make-up kit at a movie Bingo game: "It's us, it's us!" Big deal. Her plans for the future always include fortunes that land in our laps from nowhere. She insists that I marry "rich": "You can love a rich man as well as a poor man." I believe it. I go along with her. That's the way to live, great expectations. Which reminds me of our unfinished set of Dickens (bought with coupons clipped out of the *Post*). We have *Little Dorrit*, *Martin Chuzzlewit*, *A Tale of Two Cities*, and *Great Expectations* in the deluxe white leatherette edition. I hate Dickens' dungeons, and all his books are prisons.

Mother washing the floors today. She won't use a mop, goes down on her hands and knees. I didn't want to be chased from room to room, so I left the house. I said I was going to look for a job and she said she didn't believe me. She wants me to go to night school and get a diploma. For what a diploma? For to be one of millions with a high school diploma? I can always say I have one or forge one at a printer. And what can I do? Nothing! With my knowledge of the alphabet which I learned in first grade (my only skill) I can qualify for filing clerk. Maybe girl messenger. I wouldn't give her my salary anyway. I'd buy art supplies, and I can do that with the money I earn from my various or not so various nefarious activities. Though, that money should remain untouchable till I arrange my getaway. I know every day that I don't belong here.

Stayed away from home for three hours. Sat in the Automat with the other patrons. Ate something every ten minutes: baked beans, ice cream, jello with whipped cream, coffee, apple-sauce cake, baked beans again, this time with franks, macaroni in casserole, carrots, spinach, ham sandwich, chopped sirloin steak, parker-house roll and butter, buttermilk, mashed potatoes, chow mein with rice, grapefruit sections, lima-bean soup, navy-bean soup with crackers, and for dessert banana short cake.

Came home with a swollen belly and cramps, but it wasn't too bad. I have great capacity for food. Mother asked, "What's the matter, you pregnant?"

"If I was, would you take care of the baby?" I asked her.

"As if I don't have enough to do," she said, thinking it was all an impossible joke. Little does she know. A baby would be nice. I love babies. If I get married I want at least six babies, all kinds, but how do I get out of this place? It's dead here. Do I have to die? The next best thing is marriage:

POEM
Marriage saves,
until it shaves.

What does that mean?

twenty-three

Dr. Reiss called me. "What's the matter you don't come to see me any more?"

"I don't have pimples any more," I told him.

"I thought we were friends," he said.

"What kind of friends?" I asked.

"Don't be a stranger. I have some new equipment you'd be interested in: beautiful instruments, masterpieces on the walls, a new scale, completely redecorated. You'd appreciate it. A girl like you appreciates. I know it. And what's wrong with a summer tan in the winter?"

"Dr. Reiss, I don't want to insult you, but I hope I never have skin trouble again. By the way, what pictures do you have on your walls?"

He became extremely sly. "My door is open, see for yourself. You'll love them. You'll admire my taste. You won't be disappointed."

"I'm disappointed already," I told him, "and I bet your taste stinks, because your breath stinks and your good will stinks." But he didn't hang up and I didn't hang up.

"Listen, Selma, I haven't mentioned it before, but you're a sick girl. You're crazy. You don't know who your friends are and you try to strangle them off. I don't offer myself up to every kid with a problem. My time is valuable, only I thought with you a little would go a long way. You need help. I recommended it to your parents a long time ago. They asked me to step in and I have, but you won't allow it."

"You're a liar!" I shouted. "You're a fucking liar! You want to lay me and you know it, only you want to play God. God doesn't need a Sperti sun lamp! He has the sun. The whole hot sun. So screw you and don't call me again or I'll go to the police and have you arrested for rape."

"Have it your own way, child, but if I may I'll

send you a tried and true prescription for life. May I?"

I don't know why I was so insulting to him. He was no worse than a lot of men that I treated a lot better. Maybe I was too close to myself lately.

"Okay," I said, "send me a prescription, but don't charge me."

"I will, dear, but take my advice if you don't take anything else from me again as long as you know me—"

"What're you talking about now?" I asked him.

"Just this. Don't have a hysterical fit like you just had in front of the wrong people. You could be put away. Far away where nobody'll care whether you bang your head against a wall or not. I think you're worth saving and I'll stick my neck out. So how about it? You want to be happy?"

I slammed the phone down in its cradle, and went to rock myself to sleep. Far from the creeps of my childhood.

The next day there arrived in the mail a curt note from Dr. Reiss written on his prescription pad. It said: "Please call for an appointment. I have what you need on special order." Signed "Dr. Reiss." Boy, was he hard up!

twenty-four

I was thinking about it. I really was: how anyone else's desperation just leaves me cold. Especially Dr. Reiss's. He'd love my goose pimples. They're in his line. He'd commercialize it: "Dr. Reiss's Goosepimpery Jam." The blurb would read: "Dr. Reiss's favorite food. For breakfast he spreads it on Britbuns with butter. For lunch he suggests a GOOSEPIMPERY sandwich on baked legloaf washed down with a cold glass of EXTRACT OF GOOSEPIMPERY. To decorate your roast, the doctor has created green glazed GOOSEGOOSE in super-colossal GOOSEPIMPERY size." All he'd have to do to cultivate his stock would be to:

1) Look at me
2) Talk to me
3) Touch me
4) Be absolutely desperate to do any of these things, and then skin me alive and be a genius and grow the skin back overnight.

Maybe I love the idea; I want to be a skin factory and feel no pain.

My Chinese fortune cookie said, "Be firm in your convictions and you will succeed." My fortune when I weighed myself said "Yes." "Yes" sounds so good-natured.

I met a college boy in the park yesterday. His name is Paul. I told him about the family. (Not everything). The more I told him the more he liked me. I became spontaneous and took a chance on putting my arm around him. Then, also on impulse, we held on to each other and rolled down the hill we had been sitting on. At the bottom he kissed me and I couldn't tear my lips away. It was like being in a romantic horror film where the girl is lying on a table next to the beast (or madman) and between them is a huge flask full of thunderous lightning: the soul of the beautiful girl is passing into the beast and the evil of the beast is passing into the beautiful girl. It was like that—a terrible transfer—a sucking of souls. His glasses fell off. That should be the signal; when someone loses his soul his glasses pop off automatically.

I went down to the lake again to see if Paul would come. He didn't. Seldon introduced me to him but I don't like to call Seldon about where Paul lives because Juanita might answer.

Well, Paul looked ME up! He honestly likes me. We went to the park and I danced for him. I swooped close to the earth like a brown tree swan (rarest of all). He just sat and stared through his goggles.

"Feel this," I said. I made him feel the muscles in my leg. "I dance on the roof every day." He was very shy and barely brushed my flesh so I took his hand and forced it all around my calf and thigh. "See?"

"I'll bet you could crack someone's ribs with legs like that."

"Maybe I could. I don't know my own power."

"Want to find out?"

Paul must have been kidding but I have a strange intuition that he would have thrown himself between my legs as a human sacrifice. There are things in Paul very religious and penance-stricken. Who knows, I may have a sinister desire to rule the world with my legs some day and then he'd come in handy.

Paul told me that he is a painter. I told him that I am a painter. He can't show me his work yet because it's locked in the basement of his house and his mother misplaced the key. Paul reads much more than I do, and he writes too. He gets stomach-aches frequently and makes fun of them; he calls them the virus *voovontzen.* I put my ear to his stomach one afternoon and could hear the *voovontzen* simmering.

We went to C&L for ice-cream cones and I paid for my own, which impressed Paul. He made me close my eyes and then kissed the eyelids. If I was blind I would see again, but since I'm not, the pressure made my eyes a little blurry.

I told mother I met a nice boy. She said, "Why shouldn't you meet a nice boy?" Tomorrow morning he'll be alone in his apartment—tomorrow morning we have a date alone in his apartment—and tomorrow, tomorrow will never come.

twenty-five

FOR LOVE OR LUST
A New Title by Silver Gems Books

I

I took a bath at six in the morning in my house on Sedgwick Avenue. By eight o'clock the same morning I found myself taking a shower in an apartment on upper Broadway. A young gentleman very much alive faced me: filter king beside the regular size. He bit my hair.

"Tastes bitter," he said.

"That's the shampoo," I told him. "Wait till it

washes out." The water cascaded over our bodies like jujubes in spring.

"Are you afraid of me?" he asked.

"No, not of you; of it," I answered.

"I promise to keep that old devil-dog of the flesh from wagging its mangy tail," he said and vigorously soaped it up and hid it from view.

"I'm cleaner than I've ever been before and it feels good," I said. "Once I thought the only way to cleanse myself was by tainting the world."

He clapped a wet hand over my mouth. "You don't have to think that way any more."

The bathroom was full of steam. It was tough to do anything but breathe in there.

And now a slight pause for the way it really was. I washed Paul as if he was a pet dog. I kept a soapy grip on him with one hand while I scrubbed away with the other, and he loved it. "I think you missed this spot," he said, pointing to his left knee. He was so hairy all over; he could have been a new science fiction character: Cocoanut Man. Cocoanut Man visits the rain forest with Selma Silver. She tips him over and drinks brain milk; it tastes soapy. When she speaks, a huge bubble surrounds them and hardens into plastic, protecting them from the rain. They kiss, but cocoanut strands catch in her teeth. Trapped together mouth to mouth, bubbles continue to issue from her with each cry for help.

The bubbles crowd them. The bubbles crush them. With her last breath, Selma Silver says, "If only they wouldn't harden, if only they'd be satisfied with a temporary shape."

Paul reached out for a towel and I dried him. Then he dried me. It was like exchanging magazines in a waiting room.

WAITING ROOM SEQUENCE

PAUL: Do you think it'll be long?
ME: It's been long.
PAUL: I'm first.
ME: I saw you when I came in.
PAUL: Look at this—
ME: What a wonderful picture.
PAUL: It's you.

"Look," I said, "how small I am compared to you. Do you think I have a nice body?"

FOR LOVE OR LUST

II

He flipped the light switch on and illuminated the jar of melting grape jelly we had been standing in. The shower curtains were lavender, the wallpaper was orchid, my blood was wine.

"You have an intelligent face," he said. "You have a straight face, you set your jaw. You're Helen of Troy. Oh you sweet-faced young female, you floor me. Then let us lay together in our strange and narrow fashion. I am your un-hero." I tried to decipher his secret message. As a trusted agent of the Amazons I should have known. Our face-to-face confrontation had not as yet yielded the important information.

"Do you live here?" I asked.

"No," he answered, "I just came in for the shower."

My pencil point keeps breaking. The breaking point. I like to stop writing and remember how it feels. I think I frightened him. Not in the shower but in bed. I hope not irrevocably. Because for a few minutes I put him in with those kind of men who use women but don't want to know them. And I just threw myself on his bed and lay there like a corpse. So what happened is nothing, which is what I wanted to happen, although we both acted very disappointed.

After thinking about Paul for two days and wondering whether he'd call, he did.

"How are you?" I asked.

"Waiting for you," he said.

"Want me to come over?"

"Yes. And by the way, you have a magnificent body."

"You're crazy."

I told mother I was going out to meet Paul. She said she'd like to invite him for dinner. He might as well know the worst. This will put him to the test.

FANTASY ON PAUL MEETING THE FAMILY

ME: Mom, this is Paul, and this is my uncle Ernie (shake of hands) and this is my dad (shake of hands) and this is my sister (tweak of breasts), her name is Lucille.

PAUL: You kroavneys may not understand me. There is a language barrier.

ME: He's kidding. He's as American as we are.

PAUL: My whole existence is a ludicrous black muck of non-being. Which means I shoulda stood in bed.

MOM: Would you like something to eat?

PAUL: Some freshly slopped brew might help. Mind if I kingfish in your bowl of Cheezits?

I whisper into his ear that he is acting disgusting. Mother catches me whispering and says, "If you have to whisper, go outside." So we go outside and wedge ourselves out of sight behind the hall door. Oversize plaster models of human ears and brains shove in with us. Paul points to the BRAIN and remarks, "This is merchandise I have been seeking for a long time." I shiver and shrug. Mother calls out after us, "What're you doing out there, making a speech? Come back in." The BRAIN speaks: "I am the gent with the R.S.V.P. Waddaya think? Should I go?" Paul leaves with vigorous knee action. The ears and BRAIN bounce after him. I exhale the words 'ego-pants' and run up the stairs two at a time. Mother is refilling the bowl with Cheezits. Uncle Ernie complains, "He left without saying goodbye." Sister Lucille says, "How can you like someone who wears glasses?" Dad says, "Next time tell him to leave his dictionary at home. I went to college too."

twenty-six

Paul's door was open. I sneaked in. It was dark in his place but he knew I was there. He must have been waiting by the elevator watching the floors change.

"Don't move!" he ordered. I moved anyway and banged my leg on a table. "I want you to hear this in the dark. It's for you. It's an entrance-exit poem. It's a verbal agreement. It comes to you directly from the rarely understood empyrean.

"Whatever thou may dream, thou art a *thing;*
Thou answerest when the phone saith ting-a-ling
(Except in dream, perhaps); thou likest Bing;
And thou dost leap our leap who common feel
the gooser's sting.
But be of cheer, Selma, in thy cell,
Our droppings all contribute to thy smell;
Thou stinkst, we think, then stink our thoughts
as well,
And we shall share our Bosco when the milkman
comes in hell."

I thought he was insulting me. Even if it's philosophical I don't want to hear that I stink.

"Where are you?" I was ready for blood.

"Did you like it?" I heard him moving toward me.

"I hated it," I said. "I don't know much about poetry but I don't want to go to hell."

"YOU ARE THERE!" He tripped me from behind and we went down on the rug struggling wordlessly for a change. It was more fun than the first time we were together. Conflict, inflict, that's the trict. I got on top of him and pretended to clunk his head on the floor, but I put my other hand under his head so it was softer than violence. (His head?)

"What's your beef?" I demanded.

"My beef is now chopped meat."

"Is that all you've got to say after almost killing

me in the dark?" He tried to sit up but I enjoyed keeping him there.

"I've got more to say," he said. "What thighs you have. You can free me."

"You're not mad any more?"

"You're the one who was mad; don't you realize what an impression you've made on me?"

"No."

Paul wants to save up money so we can go live together. I'm sitting here and he's sitting at his job drying movie stills. It is midnight, the witching hour, and this young witch is mounted on a smooth broom flying through the air.

BROOM: Where to, oh witch?
ME: Take me to Paul.
BROOM: Where is he?
ME: East of the Sunday and west of the Moondog. But you must land silently and invisibly; he is concentrating. You cannot miss him. He is seated at one end of a long line of rollers and squeezers waiting for the photos to come out. (Oh that feels good—the wind is lifting us.) If they're not dry enough he puts them through the rollers again. He may be half asleep. All night long he examines damp scenes of love, violence, and fantastic, indescribable monsters ravaging cities.

It is a labor of love. He says he is presiding over priceless artifacts of our civilization, but I believe he is bewitched. I must break the spell and get him to take a daytime job.

BROOM: Beware, young mistress, and remember this rhyme:

The day the day is on the way,
The night the night is out of sight,
use your flashlight.

ME: You're a wise old broom and I'll never use you to sweep the floor.

There are about as many 'reasonable' apartments as there are reasonable people. And the 'reasonable' ones are usually crummy. We looked at one near the East River Drive. The door opened almost directly into the toilet which was a water closet that resembled a faded cedar chest anchored to a porcelain boatub. (Your palanquin, m'lady.) If I happened to make a wish while eating in that kitchen, it would be an accomplishment of ease and beauty to throw pennies into the toilet and make the wish come true. Another feature of the apartment was the Indian balance-your-weight-evenly room. Splinters stood up like nails all around the bedroom floor. Sharp as swords, they would have to be mown down like an evil nuptial guard, and then the area cared for like a monument. (They died for us so that we could screw.) While we were deciding whether or not we wanted to live there, the janitor smashed a roach on the wall with his bare hands. Paul admired this demonstration, but I almost threw up when I saw the creamy smear it left.

I don't know if I want to put myself into the hands of a stranger (Paul). I'm scared. What if I have to go to work? What if he falls in love with a photo? What if I have to stay appealing every day? When my panic is over I know just what I'll do: go south and make myself a beauty. I'll return wrapped in tan like a carmallow. Then, when Paul peels my wrapper off, the sweet taste of fresh Selma should make him crave me forever.

The text is set in 11 point Monticello
with 4 points of leading. This face was issued
by the Linotype Company only a few years ago,
but it is based on type made in 1796 by
Binney & Ronaldson of Philadelphia.
It has a distinctive personality with some
curious and subtle features. Perhaps
less subtle, but no less distinctive, is
the chapter heading type—Greco Bold Italic.
The composition, printing, and binding
are by H. Wolff Book Mfg. Co., Inc. The paper
is Tileston and Hollingsworth Antique.

Design: MARSHALL LEE